D0193063

CRISPIN

THE CROSS OF LEAD

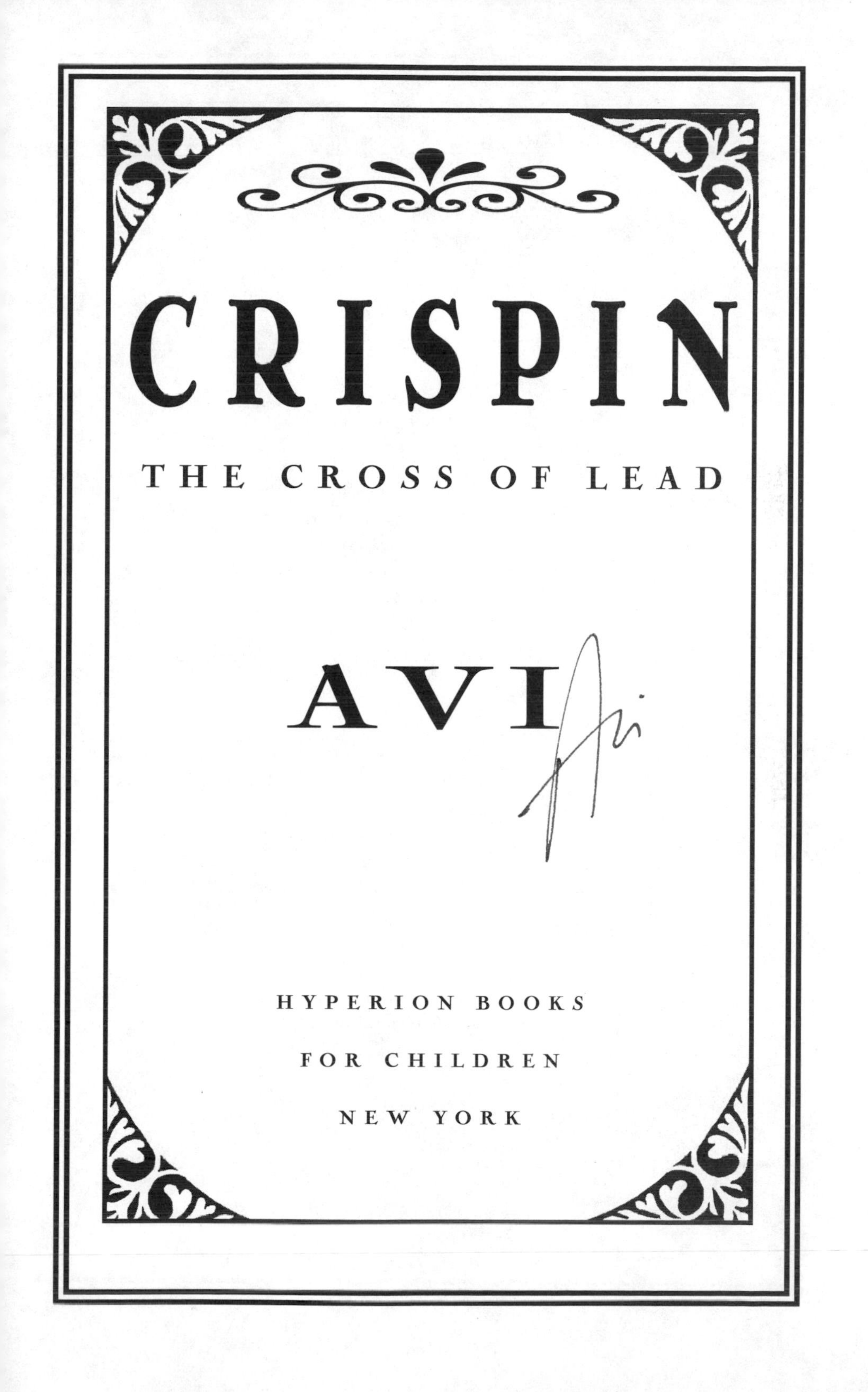

CRISPIN

THE CROSS OF LEAD

AVI

HYPERION BOOKS
FOR CHILDREN
NEW YORK

For information address Hyperion Books for Children,
114 Fifth Avenue, New York, New York 10011-5690.
First Edition
1 3 5 7 9 8 6 4 2
Printed in the United States of America
Library of Congress Cataloging-in-Publication Data
Avi, 1937–
Crispin: the cross of lead / Avi.— 1st ed.
p. cm.
Summary: Falsely accused of theft and murder, an orphaned peasant boy in fourteenth-century England flees his village and meets a larger-than-life juggler who holds a dangerous secret.
ISBN 0-7868-0828-4 (hardcover : alk. paper) — ISBN 0-7868-2647-9 (library : alk. paper)
[1. Identity—Fiction. 2. Orphans—Fiction. 3. Middle Ages—Fiction. 4. Great Britain—History—Edward III, 1327–1377—Fiction.] I. Title.
PZ7.A953 Cr 2002
[Fic]—dc212001051829

Visit www.hyperionchildrensbooks.com
For more information about Avi and his books, visit www.avi-writer.com

To Teofilo F. Ruiz

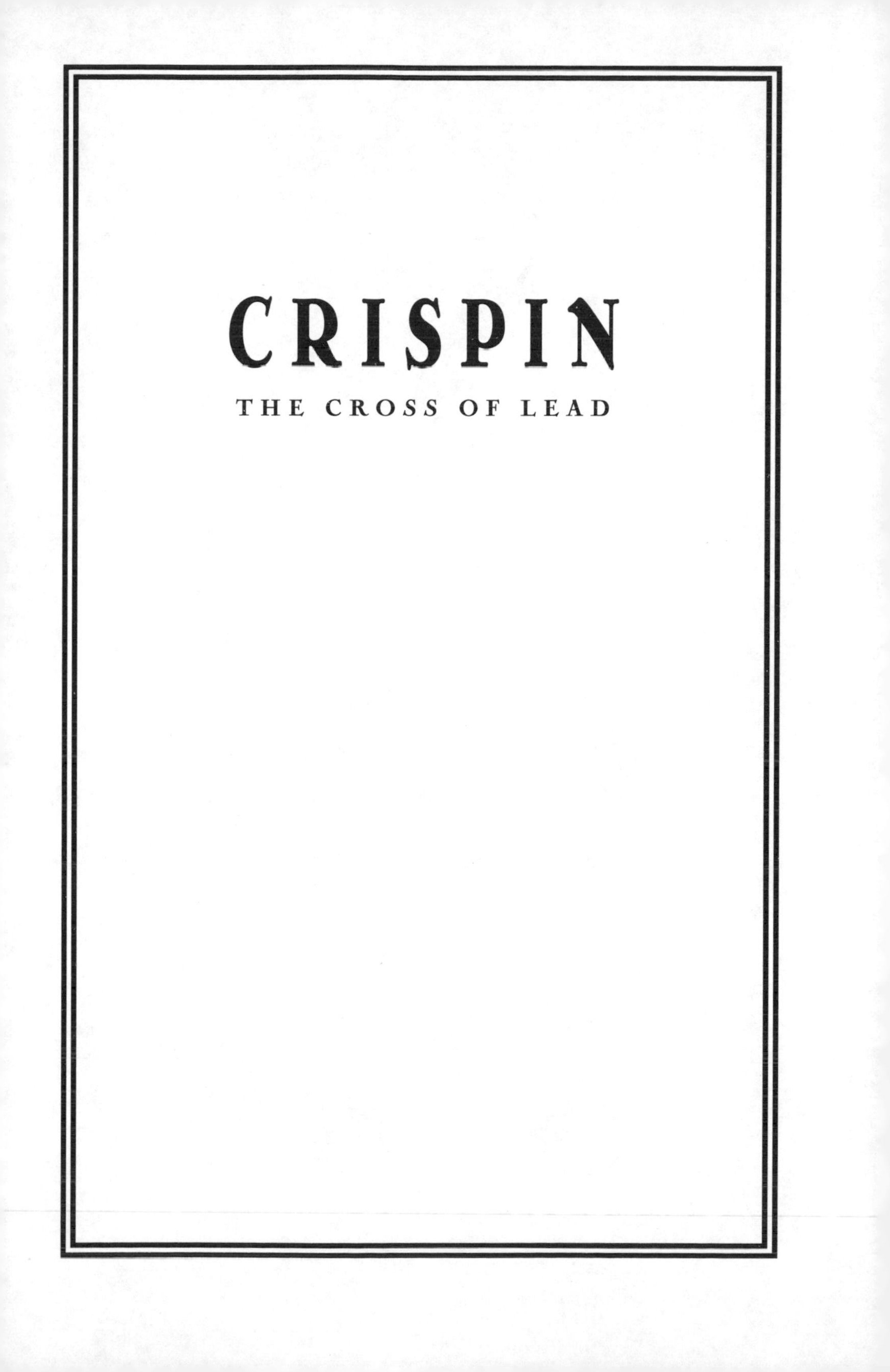

CRISPIN

THE CROSS OF LEAD

ENGLAND, A.D. 1377

"In the midst of life comes death." How often did our village priest preach those words. Yet I have also heard that "in the midst of death comes life." If this be a riddle, so was my life.

1

HE DAY AFTER MY MOTHER died, the priest and I wrapped her body in a gray shroud and carried her to the village church. Our burden was not great. In life she had been a small woman with little strength. Death made her even less.

Her name had been Asta.

Since our cottage was at the village fringe, the priest and I bore her remains along the narrow, rutted road that led to the cemetery. A steady, hissing rain had turned the ground to clinging mud. No birds sang. No bells tolled. The sun hid behind the dark and lowering clouds.

We passed village fields where people were at work in the rain and mud. No one knelt. They simply stared. As they had shunned my mother in life, so they shunned her now. As for me, I felt, as I often did, ashamed. It was as if I contained an unnamed sin that made me less than nothing in their eyes.

Other than the priest, my mother had no friends. She was often taunted by the villagers. Still, I had thought of her as a woman of beauty, as perhaps all children think upon their mothers.

The burial took place amongst the other paupers' graves in the walled cemetery behind our church. It was there the priest and I dug her grave, in water-laden clay. There was no coffin. We laid her down with her feet toward the east so when the Day of Judgment came she would—may God grant it—rise up to face Jerusalem.

As the priest chanted the Latin prayers, whose meaning I barely understood, I knelt by his side and knew that God had taken away the one person I could claim as my own. But His will be done.

No sooner did we cover my mother's remains with heavy earth than John Aycliffe, the steward of the manor, appeared outside the cemetery walls. Though I had not seen him, he must have been watching us from astride his horse.

"Asta's son, come here," he said to me.

Head bowed, I drew close.

"Look at me," he commanded, reaching down and forcing my head up with a sharp slap of his gloved hand beneath my chin.

It was always hard for me to look on others. To look on John Aycliffe was hardest of all. His black-bearded face—hard, sharp eyes and frowning lips—forever scowled at me. When he deigned to look in my direction, he offered nothing but contempt. For me to pass near was to invite his scorn, his kicks, and sometimes, his blows.

No one ever accused John Aycliffe of any kindness. In the absence of Lord Furnival he was in charge of the manor, the laws, and the peasants. To be caught in some small transgression—missing a day of work, speaking harshly of his rule, failing to attend mass—brought an unforgiving penalty. It could be a whipping, a clipping of the ear, imprisonment, or a cut-off hand. For poaching a stag, John the ale-maker's son was put to death on the commons gallows. As judge, jury, and willing executioner, Aycliffe had but to give the word, and the offender's life was forfeit. We all lived in fear of him.

Aycliffe stared at me for a long while as if in search of something. All he said, however, was "With your mother gone you're required to deliver your ox to the manor house tomorrow. It will serve as the death tax."

"But . . . sir," I said—for my speech was slow and ill formed—"if I do . . . I . . . I won't be able to work the fields."

"Then starve," he said and rode away without a backward glance.

Father Quinel whispered into my ear: "Come to church, Asta's son. We'll pray."

Too upset, I only shook my head.

"God will protect you," he said, resting his hand on my shoulder. "As he now protects your mother."

His words only distressed me more. Was death my only hope? Seeking to escape my heart's cage of sorrow, I rushed off toward the forest.

Barely aware of the earth beneath my feet or the roof of trees above, I paid no mind into what I ran, or that my sole garment, a gray wool tunic, tore on brambles and bushes. Nor did I care that my leather shoes, catching roots or stones, kept tripping me, causing me to fall. Each time I picked myself up and rushed on, panting, crying.

Deeper and deeper into the ancient woods I went,

past thick bracken and stately oaks, until I tripped and fell again. This time, as God in His wisdom would have it, my head struck stone.

Stunned, I lay upon the decaying earth, fingers clutching rotting leaves, a cold rain drenching me. As day-light faded, I was entombed in a world darker than any night could bring.

2

ONG PAST THE HOUR OF Compline, the last prayers of the night, a sound aroused me to a confused state of wakefulness.

Because of the utter darkness and the painful throbbing in my head, I knew not where I was. Though unable to see, I could smell the air and realized I wasn't at my home. Nor was I in the fields where I often slept with the ox. Only when I sniffed again did I become sure of the woodland smells and cloying air. The rain had ceased, but it was as if night itself had begun to sweat.

Then, in a burst, I recalled my mother's death and

burial, my leaving the cemetery and the priest, my plunge into the woods. I remembered tripping, falling.

Putting a hand to my forehead, I felt a welt and a crust of hardened blood. Though my touch made me wince, the pain banished the remaining dizziness. I realized I was in the forest and lost. My tunic was cold and wet.

Lifting my head, I looked about. Midst the tangle of trees, I saw a flickering light. Puzzled, I came up on my knees to see better. But save that flame, all was murk and midnight mist, and silence lay as thick as death. In haste, I made the sign of the cross and murmured protective prayers.

Mind, godly folk had no business beyond their lawful homes at such a time. Night was a mask for outlaws, hungry wolves, the Devil and his minions. Then who or what, I asked myself, had caused the sound that had brought me to my senses?

It was my curiosity—another name, my mother had often said, for Satan—that made me want to see what was there. Despite fear of discovery, I crept through the woods.

When I came as near to the light as I dared, I raised my head and tensed my legs, ready to flee if necessary.

Two men were standing in a clearing. One was John Aycliffe. In one hand he held a fluttering torch. As always, a sword was at his side.

The second man I'd never seen before. Dressed like a gentleman, with a face of older years, he wore a hood attached to a flowing cape that hung down behind his legs. Gray hair reached his shoulders. His blue over-tunic was long, quilted, and dark, with yellow clasps that gleamed in the torchlight.

Within the circle of light I also saw the fine head of a horse. I assumed it was the stranger's.

The two men were talking. Straining to listen, forgetful of the danger, I rose up from the bushes where I hid.

As I looked on, the stranger pushed aside his cape and brought forth a wallet. From it he drew a parchment packet affixed with red wax seals. He handed it to Aycliffe.

The steward unfolded it. The parchment was wide and filled with what looked like writing. Three more red seals and ribbons dangled from the bottom edge.

Passing the stranger the torch so he could see better, Aycliffe took up the document and cast his eyes over it.

"By the bowels of Christ," I heard him exclaim even

as he made the sign of the cross over his chest. "When will it happen?"

"If God wills, it will come soon," the stranger said.

"And am I to act immediately?" Aycliffe asked the man.

"Are you not her kin?" the stranger said. "Do you not see the consequences if you don't?"

"A great danger to us all."

"Precisely. There could be those who will see it so and act accordingly. You'll be placed in danger, too."

As a frowning Aycliffe began to fold the document, he turned away. When he shifted, he saw me.

Our eyes met. My heart all but stopped.

"Asta's son!" Aycliffe cried.

The stranger whirled about.

"There!" the steward shouted, pointing right at me. Throwing the document aside, he snatched back the torch, drew his sword, and began to run in my direction.

Transfixed by fear, I stood rooted to the spot. Not until he came close to me did I turn and flee. But no sooner did I than I became ensnared in brambles that caught me in their thorny grasp. Though I struggled and pulled, it was to no avail. I was too well caught. All the while Aycliffe was drawing closer, his face filled with hate. When he drew near he lifted his sword and swung it down.

In his haste, the sword's descending arc missed me, but cut the brambles, so that I could rip myself away before he could take another stroke.

I ran on.

Aycliffe continued to pursue me, sword and torch up. He would have caught me if I had not, in my blind panic, tumbled over a cliff. Though of no great height, it took me by such surprise I went hurtling through the air, crashing hard upon my side and rolling farther down a hill.

I was stunned, my breath gone, but I had enough sense to roll over and look back. Above me—at some distance—I saw Aycliffe's torch, and his face peering down.

When I realized he had no idea where he was, I dared not move. When his light finally retreated did I pick myself up and flee.

I ran as far as strength and breath allowed, halting only when my legs gave out. Then I threw myself upon the ground, gasping for breath.

For the remainder of the night I found little rest. Not only was I in fear of being found and made subject to the steward's wrath, I was still engulfed by grief at my mother's death. Then, too, I had turned from the priest when he had asked me to church. I had broken the curfew, too. Why, I'd even stolen church wine to ease my mother's pains before she died. In short, I was certain God was punishing me.

Even as I waited for His next blow, I sought, with earnest prayers, forgiveness for my sinful life.

3

HAT LIFE OF MINE BEGAN on the Feast of Saint Giles in the Year of our Lord 1363, the thirty-sixth year of the reign of Edward the Third, England's great warrior king. We resided in Stromford Village, with its one hundred and fifty souls.

For as long as I could recall, my mother had simply called me "Son," and, since her name was Asta, "Asta's son" became my common name. In a world in which one lived by the light of a father's name and rank, that meant—since I had no father—I existed in a shadow. But he, like so many, had died before my birth during a recurrence of the Great Mortality (often called the Plague)—or so my mother had informed me. She rarely mentioned him.

Nor did she ever take another husband, a circumstance I did not question. It would have been a rare man who would want so frail and impoverished a woman for a wife. For in the entire kingdom of England there could have been no poorer Christian souls than my mother and I.

I had few friends and none I completely trusted. As "Asta's son," I was oft the butt of jests, jibes, and relentless hounding.

"Why do they taunt me so?" I once asked Father Quinel during one of my confessions. These confessions were numerous, since I had become convinced there was some sin embedded in me, a sin I was desperate to root out.

"Be accepting," was the priest's advice. "Think how our Blessed Christ was taunted on His cross."

I did try to accept my life, but unlike our perfect Jesus, I was filled with caution and suspicion, always expecting to be set upon or mocked. In short, I lived the life of the shunned, forever cast aside, yet looking on, curious as to how others lived.

There was little my mother or I could do about our

plight. We were not slaves. But neither were we free. The steward, John Aycliffe, never lost an opportunity to remind us of the fact that we were villeins—serfs—bound to Furnival, Lord of Stromford Village.

Yet this Lord Furnival had fought in France or had been off to mercenary wars for so many years that most villagers, including myself, had never set eyes on him.

It did not matter. Spring, summer, and fall—save certain holy days—my mother and I, like every other Stromford villager, worked his fields from dawn to dusk.

When winter came, we fed the animals—we had an ox, and now and then a chicken—gathered wood and brush for heat, slept, and tried to stay alive.

At a time when bread cost a quarterpenny a loaf, the value of my mother's daily labor—by King Edward's royal decree—was a penny each day, mine but a farthing.

Our food was barley bread, watered ale, and, from time to time, some cooked dried peas. If good fortune blessed us there might be a little meat at Christmastide.

Thus our lives never changed, but went round the rolling years beneath the starry vault of distant Heaven.

Time was the great millstone, which ground us to dust like kerneled wheat. The Holy Church told us where we were in the alterations of the day, the year, and in our daily toil. Birth and death alone gave distinction to our lives, as we made the journey between the darkness from whence we had come to the darkness where we were fated to await Judgment Day. Then God's terrible gaze would fall on us and lift us to Heaven's bliss or throw us down to the everlasting flames of Hell.

This was the life we led. It was no doubt the life my forefathers had led, as had all men and women since the days of Adam. With all my heart I believed that we would continue to live the same until Archangel Gabriel announced the end of time.

And with my mother's death, it was as if that time had come.

4

OLLOWING MY ESCAPE FROM John Aycliffe and my night of forest hiding, it was the sound of a tolling bell that woke me. Dawn had come, and the Stromford church was announcing early morning prayers, Prime.

In haste, I made the sign of the cross over my heart, offered up my daily prayer, and listened closely. All I heard was the sound of the bell and muted forest babble—nothing to alarm me.

Once awake, however, I could only think of what I'd seen the night before, the meeting in the woods of the steward and the stranger. Nor could I remove from my mind the steward's hateful look when he brought down his sword with the clear intent of killing me.

Even so, I tried to convince myself that it would not matter. In the past Aycliffe had treated me badly. His attack on me the night before was not that great an exception. Why should he, I told myself, be concerned that I, a nobody, had seen him at his forest meeting? It seemed my best course of action would be to return to my home and act as though nothing untoward had occurred.

With the coming of morning's light it took little to determine where I was. I made my way toward the village.

Since my mother had been a cottar—one who held no land in her own right—she and I lived in a rented one-room dwelling that stood at the far edge of our village by the northern boundary cross. A thin thatch roof kept out most rain. Earth was our floor. And since it was at some distance from the village, I was able to remain hidden from those who had already gone to their daily labor.

I was just about to emerge from the woods and run toward our hut when I caught sight of the bailiff, Roger Kinsworthy, and the reeve, Odo Langland. Not only were they carrying pikes and axes, they were heading for my cottage.

Unsettled, I drew back quickly and concealed myself behind some bushes to observe their intentions as they entered our small building. Perhaps they were looking for me, because they emerged in moments. But then, to my great shock, they began to use their tools to pull the structure down.

The cottage, being of small, mean construction, could not withstand their assault. Within moments it was little more than a heap of thatch, wattle, and clay. Not content with that, Kinsworthy produced a flint from his wallet, struck sparks, and set ablaze the place I had called my home for thirteen years.

Deeply shaken, I fled back to the forest. As I went, I kept asking myself why they should have done such a thing. I could not believe it was merely because I'd seen the steward in the forest the night before.

Once within the woods, I decided to go to a high rock which stood near the forest edge and overlooked our village. Though the rock was difficult to climb, I'd done so before on one of my solitary rambles. It was to be hoped that I'd see something to help me understand what was happening.

It was not, however, till midmorning—which I knew by the position of the sun and the ringing of the church bell proclaiming Terce—that I reached the rock.

Once having made sure I was alone, I climbed. While the rock was not an easy ascent—at some places it was little less than a cliff—I reached the pinnacle. Once there I took the further precaution of lying down. Only then did I lift my head and look about.

Before me—like some rolled-out tapestry—was my entire world, beneath a sky as blue as Our Lady's blessed robes, a contrast to the greening spring that lay abundant everywhere. Overhead, swallows flitted, free as birds ever are.

To the west meandered the river Strom, glittering like a silver ribbon in the golden sun. At this point the river ran at a shallow depth. Like most, I could not swim, but for much of the year, one could wade across. Above and below this ford, depending on the season, the water ran quite deep.

A few paces from the river's bank, on the village side, stood one of the stone crosses that marked Stromford's western limit. Covered by mystic markings, this cross had been erected where Saint Giles had once appeared.

There, on the river's low, tree-lined banks, stood our noble's house—Lord Furnival's manor—the grandest house I knew. It was where the steward had lived for many years in the absence of the knight.

With stone walls two levels high and small windows, the manor was to me like a castle, high, mighty, and impenetrable. Inside—I had never been allowed to enter, but I'd been told—was an arched hall with a long trestle table and benches, several sleeping rooms, and a chapel. On the walls hung pictures of saints along with ancient battle shields. The lower level was a large storage place meant for the wheat and other foods the village produced.

Opposite the manor house, across a road, was the mill. Smaller than Lord Furnival's dwelling, it was built of stout timbers, with grinding wheels of massive stone. These wheels were turned by river water delivered by a run.

Not only did the mill grind our wheat and barley—at a cost—it contained the ovens where we villagers, by the steward's decree, baked our bread, which required yet another fee.

A road led from the riverbank. Once a traveler had crossed the river, a road lead east and reached another road that ran north and south. Where these roads met, our stone church, Saint Giles by-the-River, stood with its ancient bell.

Above and below the church were our dwelling places, some forty cottages and huts of wattle and daub, thatch and wood, dirt and mud, all in varying shades of brown.

North of the village was the commons, where we peasants grazed our own oxen and sheep. Here too were the archery butts where men of age were required, by King Edward's decree, to practice every Sunday. It was also the place where the public stocks and gallows stood.

The land for growing crops was laid out in long, narrow strips. One of three strips was planted with barley; another, wheat. The final third lay fallow for the grazing of the manor's cattle.

As for the two roads that passed through Stromford, all I knew was that they led to the rest of England, of which I had no knowledge. And beyond England, I supposed, came the remaining world: "Great Christendom," our priest called it. But in all my life I'd never gone past the boundary crosses, which marked the limits of our village.

Everything—from the woods, the cottages, the manor house, the mill, the roads, the growing lands, the commons, even the church itself, to the tiny crofts behind our cottages used for planting herbs and roots—*everything* belonged to Lord Furnival, who held it in the King's name.

Indeed, the steward said *we* belonged to our lord as well. Like all villagers, we were required to ask the steward's permission to be excused from work if ill, to grind our wheat, or bake it, to buy or sell, to travel from our parish, to marry, even to baptize our children.

In return we gained two things:

When we died there was a hope of Heaven.

And Lord Furnival protected us from the Scots, the French, the Danes, and the wicked infidels.

But that morning I had little doubt: I'd never be protected again.

5

S I GAZED FROM THE HIGH rock, all seemed calm, and completely normal. Men, women, and children were in the fields at their lawful labor, plowing, weeding, sowing, where they would remain till dusk.

But as I watched, I saw two horses with riders emerge from the manor house. By the way one of the riders sat—not well—I was sure it was John Aycliffe, the steward. The other man, I supposed, was the one I'd seen with him the night before.

The two rode slowly to the church, dismounted, and then went inside.

I waited.

The church bell began to ring. It was not the slow, rhythmic pealing that announced the canonical hours, but a strident, urgent clamor, a call to important news.

In the fields, people stopped their work and looked about. Within moments, they began to walk toward the church. Others emerged from cottages. It did not take long before the entire village was assembled in front of the church porch. Once all had gathered, the bell ceased to ring.

Three men stepped from the church. The first to come was the steward. Then the stranger. The last was Father Quinel, whom I recognized because old age had marked him with a stoop.

The trio placed themselves before the doors of the church where the steward briefly addressed the crowd. Then the stranger held forth at greater length.

Finally, Father Quinel spoke. Then, followed by the steward and the stranger, as well as all the villagers, he led the way back into church.

The church bell now began to toll again, as if a Mass were being announced. But for whom or what purpose I could not guess.

I was tempted to go forward. But my apprehension—greatly increased by the destruction of my home—kept me back. Instead, I bowed my head in prayer: "O Great and Giving Jesus, I, who have no name, who am nothing, who does not know what to do, who is all alone in Thy world, I, who am full of sin, I implore Thy blessed help, or I'm undone."

6

IN TIME, PEOPLE EMERGED from the church. Most went their several ways, some back to the fields, others to their cottages. Others remained in groups, gossiping, or so I supposed. I'd have given much to hear their words.

As for the steward and the stranger, they remounted their horses and retreated to the manor house. Some of the village men went along.

Once more I had to decide what to do. I thought of going to the village for help, but there was only one person whom I could trust: Father Quinel. Had not my mother trusted him? Had not he, alone in the village, treated me with some kindness?

Even as I decided to speak to him, I saw the steward and the bailiff emerge from the manor house, along with men from the village. They were armed with glaives—long poles with sharp blades attached—as well as bows. I even saw a longbow. Just to see them made me know my worst fears had come true: a hue and cry had been raised against me.

Clinging to the rock, I watched the search party for as long as I was able. But when they became hidden by forest cover, it was time for me to flee. My visit to the priest would have to wait until the night.

7

Y DAY WAS SPENT IN A hiding game. Even though I was hunted in many places, the merciful saints were kind. I was not caught.

The searchers did come close. Once, twice, I could have touched their garments as they passed. On one such occasion, I learned enough to confirm my worst suspicions.

It fell out this way: late in the day I had climbed into a great oak so thick with leaves it hid me completely. Below, passing, then pausing, were two men.

Matthew was a stout, honest fellow known for his skill with the glaive. Luke was a small, wiry man, considered Stromford's finest archer. Both men lived near the mill.

Pausing beneath the tree in which I hid, I heard Matthew say, "I don't think we'll find the boy. He'll have gone leagues by now."

Then Matthew, shaking his head, said, "There's a kind of strength in lunacy. I've seen it before. And the steward says it was madness over his mother's death that caused the boy to break into the manor house and steal his money."

When I, in my high perch, heard these words, I could hardly believe them: I was being accused of a theft I had not done.

"So it's said," Luke replied, but not, I thought, with much conviction.

For a moment neither spoke.

Then Matthew, in a low, cautious voice, said, "If you believe it. Do you?"

I held my breath as Luke took his time to answer. Then he said, "Do I think that Asta's son, a boy of thirteen—who's as skittish as a new chick—entered the steward's home, broke into the money chest, and ran off into the forest? Ah, Matthew, I'm sure marvelous things happen in this world. I've seen a few of them myself. But no, by the true cross, I don't believe he did such a thing."

"Nor do I," Matthew said with greater strength. "But the steward says it's so."

"And that's the end of it," Luke added with a sigh.

Then they spoke bitterly of the things the steward had done: how he had increased their labors, imposed countless fines, taken many taxes, increased punishments, and, all in all, limited their ancient freedoms by being a tyrant in the name of Lord Furnival.

Luke spat upon the ground and said, "He's no kin of Lord Furnival. Only of his wife."

To which Matthew added, "God grant our lord long life so he may visit us soon and we might put our petitions before him."

Both men crossed themselves. Having spoken, they drifted off.

I'd listened to such talk before, but always whispered. People often complained about their lives, taxes, work, and fees. Indeed, there had been so much talk that the steward—who must have heard of it—called a moot and informed one and all that such speech went against the will of God; our king; and our master, Lord Furnival. That henceforward he would treat all such talk as treason, a hanging offense.

Knowing these things could not be changed—despite the words of men like Matthew and Luke—I cared little for such matters. But in learning that I was being blamed for a crime I had not done, my incomprehension as to my plight only grew.

The rest of the day I spent hiding, not even daring—despite my hunger—to search for food. Instead, I waited for darkness, past Vespers and beyond, choosing not to stir until I heard the church bell ring the last prayers of the night, Compline. Still I held back, for fear of being seen.

But once the day was truly over, when the curfew bell had rung and all lay still as stone, I crawled from my hiding place.

The night was intensely dark. Low clouds hid the moon and stars. The air was calm, though animals' slops and whiffs of burning wood made it rank. No lights came from the village but some gleamed in the manor house.

Only then did I creep toward the church, alone, uncertain, and very full of fear.

8

ATHER QUINEL LIVED BEHIND our stone church in an attached room without windows. Though I saw no light beneath his door—one of the few doors our village boasted—I knocked softly.

"Who's there?"

"It's me, Father Quinel. Asta's son."

A slight sound came from within. The door pulled open. The priest's small, pale face peered out. His once-white alb, which covered him neck to foot, seemed ghostlike.

Frail from his many years, Father Quinel had served in Stromford his entire life. Now he was small and wizened, with sparse gray tonsured hair. Some claimed he was the unwanted son of the previous Lord Furnival, who had provided him with the church living when Quinel was still a boy.

"God be praised. Is that truly you?" he whispered.

"Yes, Father," I said, adding quickly, "and I didn't steal that money."

He made the sign of the cross. "Bless Jesus to hear

you say it. I didn't think it likely." Clutching me with his trembling, bony hand, he said, "Come quickly. The church will be safest. You're being looked for everywhere. I have some food for you. If anyone comes, claim sanctuary."

He led me inside the church. A large building, it took a man standing on another's shoulders to reach the pointed roof. Some said it was as old as the world, built when our Blessed Savior was first born. Not even Goodwife Peregrine—who was the oldest person in our village—knew for sure.

The church contained a single, open space where we villagers knelt on the rush-strewn floor to face our priest and altar during mass. Above, in deep shadow, was the carved crucifix—Jesus in His agony. Below Him—on the altar—stood the fat tallow candle, whose constant fluttering flame shed some light upon the white walls of painted lime. The font where our babes were baptized was off to one side.

Two faded images were on the walls: one was of our Blessed Lady, her eyes big with grief, the tiny Holy Child in her arms. The other revealed Saint Giles, protecting the innocent deer from hunters, a constant reminder as to what our faith should be. Since I was born on his day, and as he was the village's patron saint, I held him for the kin I never had. When no one else was there, I would creep into the church to pray to him. I wished to be the deer that he protected.

Near the altar the priest genuflected. I did the same. Then we knelt, facing each other. "Speak low," he said. "There's always Judas lurking. Are you hungry?"

"Yes, Father," I murmured.

From behind the tattered altar cloth he produced a loaf of barley bread and gave it to me. "I was hoping you would come," he said.

I took the heavy bread and began to devour it.

"Where have you been?" he asked.

"In the forest."

"Did you know they've been searching for you?"

My mouth full, I nodded.

"Aycliffe claims you stole money from the manor."

"Father," I said, "in all my life, I've never even been in there."

"I don't doubt you," the priest said, gently putting his hand to my face to keep me calm. "Most people in the village don't believe the accusation, either. But why does Aycliffe put your name to the crime?"

I told the priest what had happened when I ran from my mother's burial—my fall, my waking to witness the meeting in the clearing, Aycliffe's attempt to kill me.

"He said none of this," the priest said.

"It's true."

"What was the thing the steward read?" the priest asked. "He never mentioned that either."

"I don't know," I said. Then I asked, "Who was the man he met?"

"Sir Richard du Brey," the priest said. "He's brought word that Lord Furnival—God keep him well—has returned from the wars. He's ill and expected to die."

"The stranger said Aycliffe must act immediately."

"About what?"

I shrugged. "He said, 'Are you not her kin? Do you not see the consequences if you don't?' To which Aycliffe replied, 'A great danger to us all.' Then the man said, 'Precisely. There could be those who will see it so and act accordingly. You'll be placed in danger, too.' It made no sense to me," I said.

The priest pondered the words in silence.

"Father," I said, "what will happen if I'm caught?"

The priest put his hand on my shoulder. "The steward," he said, "has declared you a wolf's head."

"A wolf's head!" I gasped, horrified.

"Do you understand what it means?"

"That . . . I'm considered not human," I said, my voice faltering. "That anyone may . . . kill me. Is that why they pulled down our house?"

"I suppose."

"But . . . *why?*"

The priest sat back and gave himself over to thought. In the dim light I studied his face. He seemed distraught, as if the pain of the whole world had settled in his soul.

"Father," I ventured, "is it something about my mother?"

He bowed his head. When he looked up it was to gaze at me. "Asta's son, unless you flee, you won't live long."

"But how can I leave?" I said. "I'm bound to the land. They'll never give me permission to go."

He sighed, reached forward, and placed the side of one frail hand aside my face. "Asta's son, listen to me with the greatest care. When I baptized you, you were named . . . Crispin."

"I was?" I cried.

"It was done in secret. What's more, your mother begged me not to tell you or anyone. She choose to simply call you 'Son.'"

"But . . . why?" I asked.

He took a deep breath and then said, "Did she tell you anything about your father?"

Once again the priest took me by surprise. "My *father*? Only that he died before I was born. In the Great Mortality," I reminded him. "But what has that to do with my name? Or any of this?"

"Dearest boy," the priest said wearily, "I beg you to find your way to some town or city with its own liberties. If you can stay there for a year and a day, you'll gain your freedom."

"Freedom?" I said. "What has that to do with me?"

"You could live by your own choices. As . . . a highborn lord . . . or a king."

"Father," I said, "that's impossible for me. I am what I am. I know nothing but Stromford."

"Even so, you must go. There are cities enough: Canterbury, Great Wexly, Winchester. Even London."

"What . . . what are these places like?"

"They have many souls living there, far more than here. Too many to count. But I assure you they are Christians."

"Father," I said, "I don't even know where these cities are."

"I'm not so certain myself," he admitted. "Follow the roads. Ask for help as you go. God will guide you."

"Is there no other way?"

"You could find an abbey and offer yourself to the church. But it's a grave step, and you're hardly prepared. In any case, you don't have the fees. If I had them, they would be yours. No, the most important thing is for you to get away."

"There's something about my mother that you are keeping from me, is there not?" I said.

He made no reply.

"Father . . ." I pressed, "was God angry at her . . . and me?"

He shook his head. "It's not for men to know what God does or does not will. What I do know is that you *must* leave."

Frustrated, I rose up, only to have the priest hold me back. "Your way will be long and difficult," he said. "If you can remain hidden in the forest for another day, I'll find some food to sustain you for a while. And perhaps someone will know the best way to go."

"As you say."

"Your obedience speaks well for you. Come back tomorrow night prepared to leave. Meet me at Goodwife Peregrine's house. I'll ask her to give you some things to protect you on your way."

I started off again.

"And," he added, as if coming to a decision, "when you come . . . I'll tell you about your father."

I turned back. "Why can't you tell me now?"

"Better—safer—to learn such things just before you go. That and my blessing is all I can give."

"Was he a sinner?" I demanded. "Did he commit some crime? Should I be ashamed of him?"

"I'll tell you all I know when you come to Peregrine's. Make sure it's dark so you'll not be seen."

I took his hand, kissed it, then started off, only to have him draw me back again.

"Can you read?"

"No more than my mother."

"But she could."

"Father, you're greatly mistaken."

"She could write, too."

I shook my head in puzzlement. "These things you say: a name. Reading. Writing. My father . . . Why would my mother keep such things from me?"

The priest became very still. Then, from his pocket, he removed my mother's cross of lead, the one with which she so oft prayed, which was in her hands when she died. I had forgotten about it. He held it up.

"Your mother's."

"I know," I said sullenly.

"Do you know what's on it?"

"Some writing, I think."

"I saw your mother write those words."

I looked at him in disbelief. "But—"

"Tomorrow," he said, cutting me off and folding my fingers over the cross, "I'll explain. Just remember, God mends all. Now go," he said. "And stay well hidden."

Filled with dissatisfaction, I stepped from the church. As I did, I thought I saw a shadow move.

Concerned that I had been observed, I stood still and scrutinized the place where I'd seen movement. But nothing shifted or gave sound.

Deciding it had been just my fancy, and in any case too upset to investigate, I made my way back to the forest, where I slept but poorly.

Why had I been so falsely accused? I kept asking myself. How could I be proclaimed a wolf's head?

Regarding my father, why had my mother told me nothing about him? And what possible matter of importance could Father Quinel reveal of that connection?

Mostly, however, I kept marveling at the priest's revelations about my mother. That she had given me a name . . . *Crispin.* It did not seem to be *me.* If true, why had she held it secret? As for her being able to read and write, surely that could not be true. But if true, why would she have kept such skills from me? In the darkness where I lay I held her cross before my eyes. Of course I could make out nothing. In any case I could not read.

If there was one person I thought I knew, depended on, and trusted utterly, it was my mother. Yet I had been told things that said I did not know her.

I hardly knew what to think. Closer to the truth, I was in such a state of wretched disorder, I did not *want* to think. The things the priest had said made my heart feel like a city under siege.

9

N THE EARLY MORNING, I climbed back on the rock to watch for any hunting party that might resume its search for me. Happily, I saw none. Not entirely trusting what I saw, I spent my day in anxious idleness, watching, dozing, searching for acorns and berries for my food.

Sometimes I prayed for guidance as my mother had done, her small cross pressed between my hands. Occasionally I would say the name *Crispin* out loud. It was rather like a new garment that replaces an old: desired but not yet comfortable.

I tried to guess what the priest was going to tell me about my father. In truth, I feared the worst: that he was an outlaw, perhaps a traitor or someone exiled from the church, a person to make me even more ashamed of myself than I already was. I even wondered if *that* was why I had become a wolf's head—because my father had been one.

But what I kept pondering endlessly were the priest's revelations about my mother.

Though the day seemed to last forever, night returned at last. When it became completely dark, I set out for the village and the church. Though upset, I was resolved to do as the priest had instructed.

The sky was clear. A slender moon was in the sky. Nothing along the way gave me pause. But no sooner did I draw near the church than a figure rose up before me. I stopped, heart pounding.

"Is that Asta's son?" came a whispered voice.

Afraid to answer, I kept still.

"It's me, Cerdic," the voice said. Cerdic was a village boy a little older than myself.

Instantly suspicious, I said, "What do you want?"

"Father Quinel told me to come," he said. "I was to say he could not meet you."

"Not meet me?" I cried.

"Instead, he said you were to follow me."

"But . . . where is he?" I said. "And why couldn't he come?"

"I don't know."

"Why did he speak to you?" I said.

"I . . . don't know that either," Cerdic stammered.

I stared into the dark. "Where am I to follow you?"

"Along the road that leads west," Cerdic said. "Father Quinel said to say it's the safest way to go."

"But he told me I was to go to Goodwife Peregrine's," I protested. "To meet him there."

"I told you: he can't."

Not certain I should trust the boy, but unsure what to do, I stood where I was.

Cerdic moved off a few paces. "Are you coming?" he called.

"I need to do as I was told," I said and set off in the direction of Peregrine's cottage.

Cerdic followed.

Peregrine was not just the oldest person in our village, she had a special wisdom for healing, midwifery, and ancient magic. The village hag, she was a tiny, stooped woman with a dull red mark on her right cheek and wayward hairs upon her chin. It was she, no doubt, who had delivered me into this world. Like others, I looked upon her with fear and fascination.

The old crone's cottage, like most other Stromford dwellings, was built with a few timbers. It had a thatched roof, and daub-and-wattle walls. There was a space to either side of the single entryway, which had no door. One side of the space was for her animals, her cow, pigs, goose, and general storage. The other side was for her living.

I came through the entryway full of foreboding. An open fire pit lay on Peregrine's side and gave the only light. Smoke thickened the air, making the herbs that hung from the rafters look like dangling carcasses. Over the fire sat a three-legged iron pot in which something cooked. The food smells made my mouth water.

"Who's there?" Peregrine called through the smoke in her rasping, broken-toothed voice.

"It's me, Asta's son."

"Is that the priest with you?"

"It's Cerdic."

"Where's the priest? I expected him."

"He told me he couldn't come," said Cerdic. He had come up close behind me.

She peered at the boy through the smoke. "Did he give a reason?"

"None."

Muttering, "Something must have happened," she looked up into my face. Her stench was strong, and I was aware of the mark on her face. "Are you ready to go?" she asked.

"The priest said I must."

"Aye. You're being hunted by many. The steward's offering twenty shillings reward for you."

"Twenty shillings!" I cried. The amount was half a year's wages. No one in the village had such a sum. "Why should he offer so much?"

"He wants you dead," she said.

"Do you know where the steward will be looking?" I said, very frightened.

Cerdic answered. "The bailiff told people he intends to go along the northern road."

"Then best to go south," Peregrine said to me.

"Are there towns or cities there?" I said.

"I wouldn't know," the old woman said. "Now, draw closer," she commanded. "The priest asked me to provide you with protection. I do it for him, Asta's boy, not you."

I stepped forward reluctantly. She reached up and dropped a thong—with a small leather pouch—about my neck. Then she spoke some words I didn't understand.

"Eat this before you go," she said, thrusting a bowl of porridge into my hand.

After putting the cross of lead into the leather

pouch, I stuffed porridge into my mouth with my fingers. Once done, I returned the bowl.

"And here," the old woman said, offering me a bag, "is some bread. It won't take you far, but it'll take you off."

As soon as I took the bag, the old woman grasped my arm with her tiny hand, pulled me to the entryway, and all but pushed me out. "God be with you, Asta's son."

She too wished me gone.

10

ON'T GO SOUTH," CERDIC said as soon as we were outside and alone.

"Why not?" I said, trying to push away my disquiet.

"It's what I told you: the steward will be looking north. Why should he have said that if he wished to keep it secret? I think he *wants* you south. Go a different way."

"But which way?" I said.

"If the steward says he's looking north, go the way they least expect, west. That's what Father Quinel said to do."

"But that would take me by the manor house," I said.

"The last place anyone would think you'd go."

Though I was not sure I trusted Cerdic, what he said made sense. But I said, "I want to go by the church first. Maybe Father Quinel's there."

"You'd better hurry."

With Cerdic at my side, I made my way through the village. For safety's sake I kept away from the road, skirting behind the cottages, moving quietly along the back lanes.

Upon reaching the church, I knocked on the door to the priest's room. When no one answered, I went into the church proper. No one was there either.

Cerdic must have sensed my thoughts. "Perhaps," he said, "he's waiting on the other side of the river. Maybe that's why he said to go that way."

Grasping at any hope, I swung round to the road and moved in a westerly direction. Cerdic stayed close. Soon Lord Furnival's manor house loomed before us. Light beamed through a window upon the road that ran before it. The light illuminated the boundary cross and I could see the mill just opposite the manor. To see the cross moved me greatly. It meant I was truly about to leave. I hesitated.

"It's the only way," Cerdic said. He made the sign of the cross over his heart.

I peered into the dark, seeing no one but praying that Father Quinel would be waiting for me across the river.

"Keep walking," Cerdic said.

I took but a few more steps when a beating sound, as if someone were striking a drum, came from behind. Startled, I halted, and peered back into the darkness.

There was still nothing to be seen, though the drum kept beating. Then I realized Cerdic had begun to back away from me. I turned to face the boundary cross again. This time I saw shadowy forms rise up from the side of the road. It was four men. They lumbered across the road, blocking my way.

"Cerdic," I called.

When he made no reply, I looked around. He was gone.

I swung back. I saw now that two of the men were armed with glaives. In another's hands I saw the shimmering glint of a sword.

I turned around to see if I could retreat, only to see four more men approach.

I had been led into a trap.

11

STA'S SON," CAME AYCLIFFE'S voice, "in the name of Lord Furnival, you're herewith charged with theft. Give way."

I was too stunned to move.

"The boy's a wolf's head!" the steward shouted. "Slay him if you can."

From either side, men ran forward.

I ran the only way open to me, toward the mill. Reaching it, I felt about its outer walls. Finding a grip, I hoisted myself up in hope of escaping by climbing and hiding. But then a great *crack* exploded a hand's breadth from my head. Twisting around, I saw an arrow imbedded in the timbers of the mill.

Faint with horror, I loosened my grip and dropped to the ground. For a moment I squatted, trying to regain my breath and wits. Hearing the men draw closer, I leaped up and scrambled around the corner of the mill.

Aycliffe urged the men on. "Hurry! He went around the mill. Head him off. He mustn't escape."

The other side of the mill was completely dark. For all I saw, I might have been blind. Sure enough, the next moment my feet slipped out from under me, and I crashed into water.

Gasping for breath, I flailed around until my feet touched bottom. The water was up to my chest. I'd dropped into the millrace, the ditch where the river water ran to turn the mill's wheels.

Knowing I was in no danger of drowning, I paused to catch my breath and listen.

In the darkness I heard the steward continually cry out while the other men stumbled about, trying to find where I was.

Deciding to use the millrace as a path, I waded forward against the water flow, knowing it would take me to the river. The farther I went, the more the tumult behind me lessened. Even so, I had little doubt they were still searching.

The press of water increased. Stopping, I grasped

the edge of the race and hauled myself out, rolled over, and hugged the ground.

I could hear the river before me. I crawled forward, making my way down a gentle slope until my hand touched water again. It was the river.

Unable to swim, not certain how deep the river was at this spot, I hugged the bank, too timid to pass over.

I spied lights upstream. They looked like torch flares. The men were hovering near the fording place, thinking I'd try a crossing there. I had to either cross where I was or go a different way.

Afraid of the river, I chose to turn and work my way back to the millrun. I slipped in, waded across, and came up on the other side. Gaining firm ground, I began to run.

I went past the cottages and across new-plowed fields until I reached the road. Not stopping, I rushed on.

In such moonlight as there was, I made my way to the southern end of Stromford and another boundary cross.

It was when I knelt down to pray that I saw a form on the ground. It took a moment for me to realize someone was lying there.

My first thought was that it was a guard meant to stand against me and that he had fallen asleep. But when the person didn't move, I drew forward, albeit timidly.

It was Father Quinel. He lay very still. "Father?" I called softly.

He did not answer.

I knelt down, reached out and touched him gently. "Father?" I said a second time.

He still did not move.

I peered closer only to see that his throat had been slit. His blood, made black by night, lay pooled upon the ground.

Stifling a shriek, I knelt down, my whole body shaking. Terrified, I made a short and desperate prayer to Saint Giles, imploring his blessings on the priest and on myself. That done, I ran away.

God, I was certain, had completely abandoned me.

12

OMETIMES I RAN, SOMETIMES all I could do was walk. All I knew was that if the steward overtook me—and he with horse—I'd not survive for long.

With every step I took, and with every look back, I shed tears of grief. That the death of Father Quinel had to do with my mother and me, I didn't doubt. I wondered if it was because the priest was helping me, or that it was because he was about to tell me about my father or something more about my mother.

I forced myself along, keeping to the road, though to speak of the muddy path I took as a *road* was a gross exaggeration. Though uneven as well as muddy, and barely half a rod across, it's what I followed.

I had gone for but a short time when I realized I'd lost the sack of food Goodwife Peregrine had given me. I halted, even considered going back to find it, but knew that would be folly. I'd have to forage as I went.

I did touch around my neck. The little pouch the old hag had given me—with the cross of lead—remained. Grateful to have that at least, I pushed on.

At first the road took me by open areas, but soon it led me into a forest of densely twisted trees that allowed neither moon nor starlight to seep through. After going a little more I halted, too exhausted to go on. I sank down, back propped against a tree.

Though worn out from my flight, my close escape,

not to mention my churning emotions, I could not rest. I kept thinking of all that had happened, trying to make sense of what had occurred, of how I had become a wolf's head. As for what *would* happen, I could see little but an early death in an unmarked grave—if I were lucky to have even that. What's more, I knew that that if I died alone, without the benefit of sacred rites, I'd plunge straight to Hell, and my torments would go on forever.

Unable to sleep, I sat midst the swarming darkness, starting at every random rustling and crackling that came to ear. Then the wind began to moan, causing branches to stir and trees to creak and knock one upon one another. These sounds were lanced by the hooting of the Devil's own bird, an owl. Far worse were the sudden silences that suggested *something* lurking near.

At length I flung myself upon my knees and prayed long and hard to Our Savior Jesus, to His Sainted Mother Mary, and most of all to my blessed Saint Giles, for mercy, guidance, comfort, and protection.

This putting myself in God's merciful hands brought me a little relief, enough to allow me to fall into an irregular sleep, unsure what the next day would bring.

13

EXT MORNING I AWOKE TO the sound of galloping hooves. Greatly alarmed, I pressed myself upon the ground and lifted my head just enough to see the road. It was John Aycliffe, the steward, as well as the man I'd seen with him in the woods. The bailiff was there too. The three went racing by, sweeping quickly out of sight.

"Thank you, Saint Giles," I whispered, "for protecting me."

In a sweat from fright, I rolled upon my back and stared into the branches above. A cold rain was falling. The light was dim.

Stiff in limb, chilled in bone, numb in thought, I shifted about. As I did, some tiny animal scurried into the underbrush. Oh, how I then wished that I could be such a wee creature, small enough to hide so well.

As I lay there, I remembered Goodwife Peregrine's pouch that hung about my neck. With a spurt of hope, I sat up, and emptied the contents into my hand. To my dismay it contained three seeds, one of wheat, one of barley, and one of oats—plus my mother's cross of lead.

Sorely disappointed, I tossed the seeds away but decided to keep the cross in the pouch as the solitary connection to my past.

If I hoped to live, I knew I could not return to Stromford. Yet my fear of the open road was just as dire. What if I were to be seen by the steward? And, beyond that, recalling Father Quinel's description of towns and cities, I was too timid to press on.

I, who had already gone farther from my home than I had ever gone before; I, whose life had become so quickly altered; I, who had never really had to make important choices about *anything*—now I had to decide everything for myself. The result was that I stayed where I was. In truth, I dreaded going far from the road lest I lose the muddy thread that connected me to the only life I knew. In faith, I did not know how to do otherwise.

Thus for the next two days I kept to the forest, only now and then meandering off at short distances in search of food. All I found were acorns and bitter roots.

All in all, I spent my time in an aimless, crushing sadness, consumed by an alternating dread and desire that

I might be caught. If I were caught, at least my misery would have ended.

It was during the afternoon of the second day that I saw the bailiff again upon the road. Alone, he was, I supposed, heading back toward Stromford.

While somewhat reassured, I wondered where the steward was. I could not help thinking he was waiting ahead for me.

But once the bailiff passed I made myself recall my mission: a need to get far from Stromford to some city or town that had its own liberties. It was what Father Quinel had told me to do.

Such thoughts forced me back upon the road, where I continued on. Sometimes I stumbled. Sometimes I sat by the roadside, head tucked within my folded arms while waiting, I knew not for what. Then yet again—pushed by the need to act—to move—to do *anything*—I went on.

Late that day, besieged by fears, very lonely and quite famished, I fell to my knees and prayed with deep-hearted, sobbing words. In these prayers I acknowledged my great unworthiness to my Lord Jesus and searched my heart for every sin to which I could confess. This time I begged Him to gather me that I might join my mother in His holy Heaven. The truth was—and how great my shame—I no longer wished to live; which was, I knew, a sin.

14

N THE THIRD MORNING OF my escape I woke to a woollike world of misty gray. Thick and clammy air embraced me like the fingers of some loathsome toad. Sounds were stifled. Solid shapes were soft as rotten hay. No sun jeweled the sky. My entire world had shrunk down to the frayed margins of the sodden road. I walked as solitary as Adam before the creation of Eve.

As I pressed on through the boundless mist, my damp feet sucking soggy soil, the road went up an incline. Suddenly, I spied what appeared to be a man hovering in the air. Heart pounding, I halted and peered ahead.

Was it a mortal? My first thought was that it was the steward. Or was it a ghost? A demon perhaps? Or was it an angel come from Heaven to take me to the safety of God's sweet embrace?

Then, with a lurching heart, I realized what it was: a dead man swinging from a crossroads gallows.

I drew close.

It was a man—for so he had once been. Now his face was moldy green and much contorted, with a protruding tongue of blue that reached his chin. One eye bulged grotesquely. The other was not there. His body oozed from open wounds. Swollen legs and arms flopped with distended disjointedness. Bare feet pointed down with toes that curled upon themselves like chicken claws. Such clothing as he wore was nothing more than a loincloth of filthy rags. Sitting on his left shoulder were blue-black crows feasting on his corruption. He stank of death.

A piece of writing was affixed to him by a broken arrow that stuck out from his body. Since I couldn't read, I had no idea what it said.

Terrified, I sank to my knees and made the sign of the cross. Perhaps there were some outlaws lurking near. Then I thought that it might be some thief brought to his lawful end. I tried to imagine what awful thing he might have done to deserve such a fate. Then with dread, it came to me that God had set the man before me as a warning. The next thought that took hold was that I *had* already died. That here were the gates of Hell.

How long I stared at the corpse, I do not know. But as I knelt, the mist seemed to ensnare my body like a sticky shroud, intent on dragging me down.

Except—as Jesus is my Savior—as sure as my heart understood anything—I knew then how much I wished, not to die, but to *live.*

I can give no explanation how I came to this understanding, save that I did not want to become the blighted man who dangled before me, pillaged by the birds.

Knowing how wondrous are the works of God, I thought that perhaps He—in His awful mercy—was speaking to me with this dreadful vision. For I knew that, from that moment on, I was resolved to stay alive.

But which of the crossroads was I to take? North, south, east, or west?

"Please, dear God," I cried aloud, my eyes streaming hot tears, "choose a path for me."

In the end I followed the path of the misty sun, which stared down at me from the gray sky like the dead man's blank and solitary eye.

15

LL THAT DAY I CONTINUED walking. Nothing blocked my way. The mist lifted. The air turned light. Still I saw no one, not even from afar. From time to time I found streams to slack my thirst but not so much as a crumb of food.

Sometimes I traveled through woods. More oft I passed abandoned fields. While I saw birds aplenty, heard them too—wood pigeons, cuckoos, thrushes—I wondered if England had no human souls. Would I find no life or food anywhere?

More than once I reminded myself of the times when my mother and I had gone without sustenance. If we could survive then—and we did—I could do so now.

During the afternoon of the following day, still going westerly and while coming off a rise, I saw ahead what looked to be a village situated in a dell. It was a cluster of cottages, and, taller than the rest, a church of stone. At first glance it seemed as if the hamlet contained fewer dwellings than my own Stromford.

Still, my heart began to race. Perhaps this was

where God had led me, where I would gain my liberties, where people would treat me kindly. And where there would be food for me.

Yet as I drew close I began to sense something greatly amiss. There was no rising smoke, no people, sheep, or cows. No living thing appeared, not so much as a single cock, goose, dog, or pig. Nor were there smells, no dung, no manure. The fields I passed had long been unplowed.

As I came into the village proper, I saw that all lay in ruin. Roofs had collapsed. Walls had fallen in. Carts and wheels were broken. Tools lay scattered on the ground. The roof thatch that remained was worn to shreds, full of gaping holes. House daubing had crumbled and remained unpatched. Wattle had unsprung. In the middle of the hamlet I came upon a well whose surface water lay thick with clotted scum.

My skin crawled with trepidation. Something ghastly had occurred. I was put to mind of my nightmarish thought, that I had come to Hell.

But gradually, I began to grasp what it was I'd come upon: the remnants of a village destroyed by the Great Plague of some years back.

In Stromford there had been much talk of this

devastating pestilence, "the Great Mortality," as it was called. Our village had lost more than half its inhabitants, some by death, others by a desperate fleeing. It had caused my own father's death.

The cause of this blight was well known: God had sent it as punishment for our sins. All one could do was pray to Jesus and run—and even then, there was no escape. As Father Quinel had always warned, God in His sweet mercy and unforgiving anger touches whom He wants. No soul can escape His wrath.

Here, not one person appeared to have remained alive. The profound stillness that embraced all was its own sad and lonely sermon.

Still, desperate to find some food—even a tiny morsel—I crept with care through what remained, fearful my steps might waken restless spirits. To protect myself, I gripped the cross of lead in my hand.

In search of food I made myself enter one of the better structures, an empty cottage with half a roof. Some of its walls remained. In a collapsed corner sat a brown-boned skeleton. About its open ribs lay shreds of old cloth. Once fair hair dangled from its skinless skull. Its fleshless hands clutched a tiny cross.

I made the sign of the cross over my own hammering heart and retreated, then rushed through the village, wanting nothing more than to flee.

But as I was passing the broken church I heard a solitary singing voice:

"Ah, dear God, how can this be
That all things wear and waste away!"

16

TARTLED, I STOPPED. THEN I became afraid. After what I had witnessed in the village, I could not believe I was hearing a *living* voice. But when the voice sang out again—and I realized it was coming from the abandoned church—I told myself that a church was an unlikely place for evil spirits to abide. Besides, food was uppermost in my thoughts, and I had desperate hopes that I might have come upon a survivor.

Trying to make no sound and clutching my cross of lead, I went around by the side of the church, where windows had once been but where only gaping holes remained. As I drew closer, the voice sang out again. This time it was accompanied by the beating of what sounded like a drum.

"Ah, dear God, how can this be
That all things wear and waste away!"

Cautiously, I peeked inside.

At first, all I saw was rubble and rot. Then, partly hidden in the shadows, I saw a man who was anything but a skeleton. On the contrary, he was a mountain of flesh, a great barrel of a fellow, whose arms and legs were as thick as tree limbs, and with a tubike belly before all. Legs extended, he was sitting with his back propped against a crumbling baptismal font. He was, moreover, garbed like no man I had ever seen before. Upon his head was a hat which seemed to have been split into two, like the points on a cock's comb. At the end of these points hung bells. Moreover, the flaps of his hat came down along both sides of his face, encircling it, then tied below, making his cheeks plump.

As for his face, most striking was a bushy beard of such ruddy red it seemed as if the lower part of his face was aflame. He also had a large, red, and fleshy nose and hairy eyebrows of the same hue, as well as a cherry-lipped mouth big even for such a face as his.

He wore a wide-sleeved tunic of black, and ankle-length hose with a different color for each leg, one blue, the other red, though the colors were faded. His brown leather boots were long and somewhat pointy at the tips. Yet, for all this rare color, his clothing was ragged, torn, and patched in many parts, enough so that I could see his dirty, hairy skin in several spots.

A bollock dagger was fastened to his hip. On the ground by his side lay a fat sack, which contained, I prayed, food.

His eyes were closed, but clearly he was not asleep. Instead, he was singing raucously while beating a small drum with his massive hands. As I looked on, he continued to tap the drum with his big fingers, bleating out his song. After repeating the words a few more times, he let loose a booming laugh as if he'd just heard a rare jest. He laughed so hard he put down his drum and opened his eyes.

Compared to the rest of him, these eyes were small and wet. Old pig's eyes, I thought, shrewd and wily. But what he must have seen was me, staring at him. For he dropped his drum and his hand went right to his dagger.

We gazed at one another in silence.

"Good morrow, lad," he cried out, even as his hand eased off his weapon. "May God keep you well."

"God be with you too, sir," I managed to say, though I was in awe of such a monstrous man.

"And where, by Saint Sixtus, do you come from?" he asked. "Not, I suppose, from this God-forsaken village."

I shook my head.

"Then what place?" he said.

"Far . . . away," I answered evasively.

"East or west?"

I pointed in the direction I had come from.

Scrutinizing me, head cocked to one side, he ruffled his beard, while a sly smile played his lips. "You have a gifted way of speech," he said. "To what purpose do you travel?"

"I'm . . . going to meet my father," I said, this being the answer I'd decided to give if asked.

"And, pray tell, does this father of yours live close?"

"In . . . some large town."

He considered me for yet a while with his shrewd, wet eyes. "So if I understand you, boy," he said at last, "you know only somewhat from where you come, but go toward . . . some other place."

"As God is true, sir."

"Do you have any idea how you look?"

"No, sir."

"Your tunic is equal parts dirt, rags, and rents. Your face is scratched and mucked as are your naked arms and legs. Your hair is long and unkempt. I can barely count your fingers for the caked filth. In short, you're more cur than boy. How old are you?" he asked. "And, as God is merciful, don't be so vague."

"Thirteen, about."

"About," he returned with something like a sneer, plus another scratch of his beard.

I said nothing, trying to make up my mind if I should run away. But, still hoping that such a barrel of a man must have some food, I stayed.

For his part, he continued to consider me steadily with his small intense eyes. "Might you," he said, as if reading my mind, "be hungry?"

My mouth began to water. "Yes, sir, as God is kind and if it pleases you."

"Hunger never pleases me," he roared. "Though our great if doddering king surely means well, his loyal subjects go hungry. And why? Because the officials of this most holy kingdom are all corrupt gluttons. His councilors and parliaments—all dressed in that new Italian cloth, velvet—sit upon the backs of the poor and eat their fill of venison and sweetmeats. Not to mention the Flemish foreigners who loot our country's gold. But such is the will of our gracious majesty, that poor souls like you and I are not part of his daily reckoning. 'It is as it is,' is *his* motto. Mine is, Let it be as it *may* be!

"What think you of *that* sermon?" he said, cocking his head, as if he really wished me to reply.

"I . . . didn't understand it," I said.

"Not at all?" he asked, showing disappointment.

"It sounds like . . . treason," I said, only to instantly regret my words.

Sure enough, his face clouded with anger. "Does it, now?" he bellowed, making me jump. "So be it. I hate all tyranny. Is *that* treason, too?"

I did not dare to speak.

Then, far softer, he said, "Well, by all the blessed saints and martyrs, what does it matter what *I* think? Come closer. I'll give you some bread."

My hunger was so great that whatever prudence I might have had, I put aside. Instead, I returned my cross to my neck pouch, and hurried around to the church's proper entry. I then approached the man where he sat, moving quickly when I saw he had untied the sack that lay by his side. With something close to elation I saw him pull up a large, gray lump of bread which he held up.

I reached out toward it.

The moment I did, his free hand shot out, and with a speed that belied his bulk, he grabbed me by my wrist and held me with the strength of stone.

17

ET ME GO," I CRIED, TRYING to pull back. "I only wanted bread."

"Bread is never free, boy," he roared. He was still upon the ground, but his arms were long, and his huge hand held me fast while the bells of his hat tinkled with the force of his exertion. "Or is it treason to say that, too?"

No matter how I tried to pry away his fingers, I could not break his grip.

"And what I'd guess," he went on, "is that you've run away from your lawful place. Out with it now, or by the wondrous music of Saint Gregory, as sure as I beat my drum, I'll beat it out of you."

"Please, sir, let me go," I screamed, for his hold was intense.

"Boy," he bellowed, "I want the truth from you, or you'll suffer from it." His fingers tightened.

"I told you, I'm going to a town."

"For what purpose?"

"To save myself."

"Save yourself?" He laughed. "No man can do so on his own. No boy, either. What makes you think you'll do it in a town?"

"I was . . . told."

"By what authority?"

"Father Quinel."

"A *priest,*" he said mockingly, gripping me tighter. "I might have guessed. And you believed him?"

"Sir, you're hurting me."

"The Devil take your hurts. Why did you run away?"

"I had to."

"Had to?" he said, his grasp so hard I thought my arm would snap.

"I . . . was proclaimed a wolf's head."

"A wolf's head. That's extreme. For what reasons?"

"My master accused me of theft."

"What master?"

"The steward. I feared he'd take my life."

"And what did you steal?"

"Nothing."

"And yet you ran away."

"To save my life, sir."

"And failed to note that anyone who catches you may haul you back?"

"Please, sir, I'm in great pain."

"And what of that father whom you seek?"

"He's dead."

"Mother?"

"Dead, too."

I no sooner said that than he released me. But in the same motion he leaped up, swung about, and stood between me and the doorway of the ruined church. My way was blocked.

18

OWERING ABOVE ME, HAT bells tinkling with mocking laughter, bushy red beard like flames from Hell, he seemed to me a true demon.

"You have a new lord now," he declared.

"Please, sir," I begged, trembling with panic and rubbing my wrist where he had squeezed it. "I don't know your meaning."

"By the putrid bowels of Lucifer, boy, the law affirms that having unlawfully left your true master, you become servant to the first free man who finds and claims you. You've left yours. And I have found you, a gift of God. From now on, you'll serve *me*."

"Please, sir," I said yet again, cringing. "I don't want to."

"You have no choice. You either do as I command, or I'll march you back to where you came from. I'm sure I'll come upon your former manor soon enough. Once there I'll toss you to your steward. No doubt he'll be pleased enough to slit your throat.

"I don't know how you came," he went on. "But did you, perchance, see that rotting man on the gallows at the crossroad?"

"Yes."

"Did you read the screed that told of his crime?"

"I don't know my letters, sir."

"Well, I do and did. That man rose up against his lord and master. How? By holding back a pound of wool to sell that he might feed his sickly child.

"What he did was *theft*," the great man said, pointing down the road, "and that's what they'll do to you for having done the same."

"Have mercy, great sir," I pleaded, dropping to my knees in terror, for he seemed to know the awful truth of things.

"Don't 'mercy' me," he thundered on, leaning over me so that I felt no more than a tiny mouse. "But swear, in Blessed Jesus' name, not to leave my side, or else your blood will flow like water. And, as God is good and holy, I promise you, in such a cursed place as this, only the dead shall know. Do it," he shouted, now brandishing his dagger.

I was in such fright I could hardly breathe. Tears were coming hard. "I . . . I swear," I choked out.

"On the sacred name of Jesus."

"On . . . the sacred name . . . of Jesus," I went on.

"That I will be your servant . . ."

"That I will be your servant . . ."

"That if I default . . ."

"If I default . . ."

The words caught in my throat. It was a dreadful thing he was making me swear. One could never break such vows.

"Say it," he cried, his dagger drawing closer.

In fear for my life, I said, "If I default . . ."

"May the all-seeing God strike me dead where I stand."

"May the all-seeing God . . . strike me dead," I whispered.

"Where I stand."

"Where I stand."

"Done," he proclaimed. Then he put his dagger aside and tossed me a piece of bread. "Now you are mine, or God will chew you up and spit you out like the living filth all wolf's heads are."

19

READ CLUTCHED IN MY trembling hand, I crept into a corner of the broken church as far from the monstrous man as I could go. Though I swallowed the bread he'd given me, I knew I'd sworn a sacred oath to which I was forever bound. Far better, I thought, to have died on the road.

Hearing him move about, I stole an anxious glance in his direction. He had sat down again, but in such a place so as to prevent me from bolting. What's more, he was staring at me with his moist, sly eyes. I dared to look back with the greatest loathing I had ever felt.

"Ah, boy, what does it matter?" he said, speaking in a far softer voice than before. "You didn't truly expect to live without a master, did you?"

I made no reply.

"Or do you believe that some day none of us will have masters?"

Unable to find words for my misery, I remained mute.

"Answer me!" he cried, making me jump. "Do you believe that someday none of us will have masters, or not?"

I shook my head.

"Why not?"

"God . . ." I said, gulping down my misery, "has willed it otherwise."

"And yet," he said, leaning toward me and leering, "when Adam plowed the earth and Eve spun, who then was the gentleman?"

His question was so unusual, I did not, could not, respond.

"You don't like my sense of humor," he said. "You think it *treasonous*."

I wanted to say *yes*, but was too afraid.

"You needn't be so resentful," he said. "When you've lived as much as I, you'll learn to neither trust nor love any mortal. Then, the only one who can betray you is yourself."

I didn't know what to say.

"Do you ever smile, boy?" he demanded. "If you can't laugh and smile, life is worthless. Do you hear me?" he yelled. "It's *nothing!*"

I winced.

Then, smiling, he cocked his head to one side, and ruffled up his beard. With a sweep of his hand, he snatched off his hat, revealing a bald pate. "By the love of Saint Arnulf the King," he said, "you could do much worse than being bound to me."

That stated, he seemed to pull back within himself and give way to private thoughts.

Fearing what sudden thing he might do next, I watched him warily. But after a while he said only, "Do you wish to ask me anything? Who I am? My name? What I'm doing here?"

"It doesn't . . . matter," I stammered.

"Why?" he said.

"Because you're already my master forever."

"So be it," he said, acting as if I had offended him.

For a while he toyed with his hat, not to any purpose that I could see, but as if lost in thought. At length, however, he reached over and took up his sack and rummaged through it. From it he took out three balls, each made of stitched leather.

To my surprise he tossed the balls into the air. Instead of falling to the ground, they stayed in the air and rotated at his will, with only the smallest touch and encouragement of his fingers.

I looked on, astonished.

"What think you of that?" he said, laughing.

"Are they . . . enchanted, sir?" I whispered.

"Hardly," he said as he continued to keep the balls in the air, sometimes higher, sometimes lower, until, as abruptly as he'd begun, he gathered them in, and they rested upon his great slablike hands.

"I'm a juggler," he said. When I made no response he said, "Don't you know the word?"

I shook my head.

"A French word. It means I balance things, or toss balls, boxes, knives—anything I choose—through the air and catch them up again. And what do I do with my skills? I wander from town to town through the kingdom. Not as a beggar, mind you, but as a man of skills. Skills, boy, which enable me to gather enough farthings and pennies to live and keep this belly full." He patted himself on his large stomach.

"Believe me," he said, "there's no place in the kingdom I've not been. Gascony, Brittany, and Scotland too, for that matter. What think you of *that*?"

He rushed at me with so many new and strange ideas I could not grasp them all. So all I said was, "I don't know, sir."

He cocked his head to one side. "Do you have *any* thoughts about *anything*?"

I hung my head to avoid his eyes.

He sighed. "What's your name?"

I hesitated, not wanting him to call me what I had always been called—Asta's son. But I was not comfortable with my newly discovered name either.

He leaned toward me, glaring. "Boy," he said, "as I am your master let me offer you advice: I'm a simple man. I go by simple means. You'll do as you're told or suffer the consequences. Now, answer me or, as there is a loving God in Heaven, I'll thrash you. What is your name?"

"I'm called . . . Asta's son."

"*Asta's son.* That's not a name. It's a description. Were you never," he said, "christened with a name of your own?"

"I was . . . told it was . . . Crispin."

"*Crispin.* That's too fine and noble a name for such rubbish as you. Have you a surname?"

"I . . . don't know."

"God's blood. You might as well have been a dog," he said.

It was all I could do to suppress screams of rage.

"Very well, Crispin—for henceforward that's what I shall call you—I too am bound for towns and cities. But I wend my way to such places—not as a runaway peasant beggar like you—but earning my bread with tossing things into the air the way I showed you. People in towns pay fair coins to see my revels in squares, in merchant houses, and inns, as well as guildhalls. Do you know how to make music?"

"Music?"

"By the Devil's own spit," he said. "Have you lived your life under a rock? Were you born of sheep? Do you know nothing of drums, horns, and pipes? Do you even sing?"

"No, sir."

"God's holy wounds," he said. "Music is the tongue of souls. Is there *anything* you can do?"

"I can follow an ox. Sow seed. Weed. Gather crops. Thresh wheat and barley."

"Merciful Heaven," he said. "And in this town or city you intended to go, were you going to plow the streets *there*?"

Unable to withhold myself I cried out, "I don't know what I was going to do. I wanted to gain my liberty. And with God's help I would have, if not for you."

His eyes opened wide. Then he tilted back his head and roared with laughter as if I had told the rarest jest of all. *"Liberty,"* he said. "And with God's help too, I'll wager. It's a marvel you don't seek out the blessed Saint Crispin himself to come to your aid. No wonder you want to die. The only difference between a dead fool and a live one is the dead one has a deeper grave."

It was as if all the scorn and insults I had ever endured were pouring forth from him. If there had been an open hole in the earth I would have crawled into it willingly.

"Ah, noble Crispin," he went on, "Our Blessed Lord, in His wisdom, must have sent you to me for instruction.

"I shall begin by teaching you something. Mark me well: with all the armies of the kingdom at your side you could not gain your liberty on your own. A boy? Alone in a city? A wolf's head? Why, any city you entered would swallow you like the whale took Jonah. And not to spit you out, either, but only to belch up your empty soul."

That said, he erupted with another great laugh. "Now, go to. Let's see if you're capable of asking me a question."

Struggling to find something, I said, "What . . . what is your name, sir?"

"Orson Hrothgar," he said. "But people call me 'Bear.' Because of my size. And strength. Pay heed, young Saint Crispin," he added, glaring at me with eyes that seemed to glint, "a bear has two natures. Sweet and gentle. If he becomes irritated, he turns into a vicious brute. So I beg you to consider the *two* sides of my nature. Next question."

"Where are you going?" I said.

"To my death," he said, "as must all men."

"And . . . before that?" I ventured.

His eyes seemed to laugh. "Ah, you do have some wit. God's truth, before I reach my end, there's work to be done. Big work. The work of ages."

"What . . . is it?"

He cocked his head and laughed. "On the Feast of Saint John the Baptist I must meet a man in Great Wexly. Large things are brewing, young Crispin," he said grandly, "and I intend to play my part. Let it be as it *may* be. But, time for that to come. Until then you and I shall wander.

Our task is to stay alive and measure this great kingdom with our feet, our eyes, our ears."

With that, he tossed his sack to me. His meaning was perfectly clear. Huge as he was, I was to carry his belongings.

Inwardly lamenting my fate, I lifted the sack and began my life as servant to the Bear. I began to wonder if he was mad.

20

HE LIFELESS VILLAGE WAS soon behind us. Bear went first, moving over the road with the strides of a giant.

And what a strange sight he was with his black tunic, legs of two colors, split hat bobbing, and bells jangling. As for me, with his heavy sack upon my back, I had to struggle to keep up.

At first we didn't speak. I was too down in my spirits. That I, in fleeing from one cruel master, should be bound to another, was almost too much to endure. And to a man who claimed he hated tyranny.

More than once I considered dropping the sack and running away. I had to remind myself that I had sworn a sacred oath to stay. To break it would cast me straightaway to Hell. There was nothing to do but march along and do as God had willed. Then I recalled that Great Wexly was one of the places Father Quinel had said I could gain my liberties. Perhaps there would be some advantage in my going there. Silently, I prayed it would be so.

For the rest of the day we tramped along. In all that time we saw no one, nor came to another village.

Once I asked, "Sir Bear, why are there no people about?"

"By Saint Roch, it's the pestilence," he said, confirming my fears. "Hardly any villages were spared in this area. But farther along, you'll see people aplenty. And in the cities . . ."

"Is there no one left in them, sir?" I asked, worried that they too might have been abandoned.

He laughed. "In London, say thirty, forty thousand."

"Forty thousand?" I cried, astonished.

"Don't worry. It's far more than any man—except

the royal tax collectors—can count. And don't call me sir," he snarled.

"Why?"

"It's servile."

"But you're my master."

His answer was a growl.

We had trudged on for I don't know how much longer when Bear stopped. "We'll take some rest here."

21

E LED US TO A GROVE OF trees. There he flung himself down and told me to do the same. That done, he called for his sack. He rummaged in it, producing more bread, which he tore and gave me half.

When we had been silent for a while—I, still brooding over my unhappy fate—he said, "I don't think you care for me."

"I have no choice," I said.

"Would you like one?"

"God's will be done," I said.

He shrugged and said, "You might not believe it, but I was fated to be a priest. In the City of York. That's far to the north."

I looked at him anew. Father Quinel was the only priest I had ever known. This huge man could not have been more different.

"It seems my father grew weary of me," Bear continued. "Said I caused too much trouble and ate too much. In truth," he added with sudden bitterness, "I suspect he offered me to God to fulfill a pledge he'd made in exchange for some profitable trade. Though, I ask you, what kind of man would exchange a boy for a sack of wool?"

His question made me think upon my father. I tried to imagine what kind of man he might have been if he had lived, and if he would have done such a thing with me.

"A punctilious man, my father," Bear went on. "He paid my fees in full, gave me his hasty blessing, and walked away. I never saw him more. Willy-nilly, I was enrolled in the Benedictine abbey to be a monk. Twelve years of age—younger than you—and already in robes. An acolyte."

"Did you become a monk?" I said.

"I was at the abbey for seven years. I learned how

to pray. How to be silent. I learned to read Latin, French, even English. There's that. It keeps me from the gallows."

"Why?" I said, for in spite of myself, I found myself interested in his story.

"The law. If you can read, you're treated as a priest. Common law does not allow priests to be hanged.

"But shortly before I took my final vows," he continued, "when on some errand for my fat and greasy abbot, I came upon a group of mummers in a square close to the York minster. Their music, tricks, and most of all, their laughter beguiled me.

"Perhaps it was the Devil himself who took a liking to my soul. In any case I ran off. Like you," he added, with a laugh.

"But . . . how could you abandon God?" I said.

"Had He not abandoned me?"

"It was your father, not God, who left you," I said.

I must have surprised him with my words, for he grew silent. And when he spoke again it was with less bravado. "For ten years I traveled with those people," he said. "They became my dearest friends. We went all about the kingdom. Mind you, we lived only a tad beyond beggary. But my companions taught me better languages: the language of song, of hand, of foot. And most of all, of laughter."

"Can you still be hanged, then?"

"Is that your hope?" He laughed. "Not as long as I can read. But I did the next-best thing. I went off to be a soldier."

"And abandoned your new friends," I said.

"Not abandoned. Disbanded. Only Saint Anthony knows where they went. Some wandered off. Others lost their lives to brawls, jails, duels, or sickness. Some were lost to marriage. The wandering life—the mummer's life—is fragile at best." He shrugged. "In any case, I'd rather be alone."

"Then, why . . . ?" I faltered.

"Why, what? Speak out."

"Then, why do you need me?" I said.

In response he reached into his sack and pulled out the leather balls again. As before, he tossed them round and round, so that they seemed to float about his hands.

"Here," he said, holding out the balls to me. "Let me see how skilled you are."

"Me?"

"Of course, you."

"I can't do such things."

"Saint Crispin," he barked, "stand before me."

Reluctantly, I took my place before him.

"Now, pay attention," he said. Beginning with one ball, he demonstrated how to toss it back and forth between his hands. He told me to do the same.

I did so, clumsily at first, but under his insistent commands, I began to grasp his method.

"There! Now," Bear said, "watch this."

He took up a second ball, and along with the first, began to throw it back and forth. "Do that," he said.

Tossing *two* balls between my hands was quite another matter. I could barely manage it.

"Again," he shouted. "And again."

When I failed he was always severe, insisting I try over and over again. But, at last, the balls began to fly for me.

After sitting back and watching me intently with his shrewd eyes, he said, "Enough. We need to move on. You'll practice more. You'll add more balls as you go. Music, too. And I vow, by the joy of Christ, you'll learn it well."

"But . . . why?" I said.

"You shall see."

We continued along the muddy road. This time, as we went, Bear sang at the top of his voice:

"Loudly sings the cuckoo!

Grows the seed and blooms the meadow!

Comes the spring,

The woods do sing!

Sing, cuckoo, now; sing, cuckoo!

Sing, cuckoo, now; sing, cuckoo!"

Then from his sack he took out a music pipe—a *recorder,* he called it—and began to play the same melody, after which he sang the verse again.

"Sing," he commanded.

"I don't know how."

"Crispin, if I bid you to sing, you'll sing," he said.

Haltingly, I tried.

"Louder."

I complied. As we went along, I was convinced more than ever that Bear was mad.

22

OWARD EARLY EVENING BEAR found a secluded spot some paces off the road. There he ordered me to stand against a tree.

I hesitated.

"Do as I say," he said.

When I did, he pulled a twist of rope from his sack, and to my alarm proceeded to tie my hands behind the tree.

"What are you doing?" I cried, seeing this as confirmation of his madness.

"I need to fetch us some food," he said, pulling the knot tight. "You'll only interfere. And I don't want you running off."

"But I swore I wouldn't," I said. "I beg you, don't leave me here."

"Pha," he mocked. "As God in Heaven knows, both wheat and trust take a full season to grow."

Without another word, he went off, leaving me alone. More than once I tested the knot, determined that despite my vow, I'd run off. But no matter how I tried, I could not get loose. Instead my arms grew numb.

How long he was gone I don't know. Enough to fill my heart with more misery and make me swear violent oaths at him. I even screamed for help, though I knew help would never come.

But when I caught sight of the sack he had left behind, I told myself he was bound to return, if not for me, for it. Sure enough, he did. What's more, a large, fat rabbit dangled from his hands.

"There, Saint Crispin," he said when he came into view, a great grin on his red-bearded face, "now you can see that for good or ill, I always keep my word."

He untied me. Faint from standing so long, my arms aching from being tied, I immediately sat down.

"Do you know the penalty for poaching?" he said as he worked his dagger skillfully to skin the rabbit.

I was so angry, I only shook my head.

"To feed us I've put both ours lives in jeopardy," he said. "That's the kind of freedom that exists in this kingdom."

With flint, steel, and tinder, he made a fire, which

he told me to stoke with bits of wood. Then he took up the rabbit, spitted it, and soon had it roasting.

"Do you like meat?" he said, seeing me with my mouth agape.

"I've only eaten it a few times," I confessed.

"A *few* times." He laughed uproariously. "Ah, Crispin, the blessed saints were kind when they guided you to me. For my part, I love meat."

When he proclaimed the rabbit cooked, he tore it apart, and gave me some. As I shoved the bits into my mouth with my hands, I admitted to myself it was the best food I had ever eaten. My resolve to flee abated—somewhat.

Later, when we had our fill—more meat than I had consumed at one time in my entire life—and the embers of the fire had burned low, Bear told me to lie down on the far side as he wished to speak to me.

What madness, I wondered, would he reveal to me now?

It had grown dark. The only light was our little fire. A breeze had sprung, which caused the flames to dance. Bear's red beard seemed to glitter in the firelight, so that his face—despite the dark—was equal to any sun. His bald head gleamed like a moon. Indeed, he was big enough to fill the entire sky.

Then he began to speak of his many adventures, his riotous life, the marvels he had seen, the scrapes he had escaped, his fortunes good and bad. Never had I heard such tales. It was a world and life, a way of being, utterly unknown to me. What's more, everything he talked about was stitched with laughter. It was as if life itself were a jest. Except, every now and then he'd cry out with an awful anger at what he called the injustices of the world.

Then he spoke of his soldiering days, fighting alongside the Black Prince in Gascony and Brittany.

"Our master has been fighting in France for so long," I said, "I've never seen him."

"What's his name?"

"Lord Furnival."

"Furnival," Bear said. "You'll be pleased to know his first home is in Great Wexly, where we're bound."

I said, "What manner of man is he?"

Bear shrugged. "I saw him too much. A great landowner. And arrogant. What he lacked in fighting skills he made up for in bragging, drinking, and killing. In that order."

"But he's a noble knight."

He snorted. "Do you think that makes him less mortal? By God's everlasting bones, Crispin, war is where the Christian is truly tested. Alas, your Lord Furnival was not one to inspire faith. If there was looting and cruelty to be done, he did more than his share. With a falcon's eyes for ransom. As for those prisoners who would yield nothing . . ." Bear waved his hand dismissively. "Doomed. Regarding his fondness for women . . . I shan't say. But you may believe me: As Jesus shall be our Judge, your Lord Furnival shall have much to answer for."

"His steward is cruel," I said.

"A suitable pair," Bear said. "And what village is that?"

"Stromford," I said before I could catch myself.

When he lapsed into silence I thought of what Bear said about Lord Furnival. It made me uneasy, thinking it might have been a mistake to reveal my connection and where I had come from. There could be a danger if Bear was truly mad and we were going there. And yet . . . he seemed to know so much, more than any man I had met. How, I asked myself, would he consider me when he knew more of what I was?

The fire smoldered. A breeze blew. A bird whistled

into the dark. My uneasiness had just begun to subside when Bear said, "Now, Crispin, it's time I learned the truth of you."

23

HARDLY KNEW WHAT TO SAY. I felt a desire to speak about who I was and what had happened. Yet it did not seem proper. He was, after all, my master. I was his servant. We were not equal.

But before I could think more on it he said, "When did your mother die?"

"A . . . short time ago," I said.

"May the blessed Saint Margaret care for her in Heaven," he said, crossing himself. "What manner of woman was she?"

Since no one had ever asked me about my mother, it was difficult to know where to begin. Just to think of her brought pain to my heart. "She was shunned by the others in our village," I said. "Nor did she talk very much. When she did, she was bitter."

"Why so?"

"I don't know. Sometimes I thought it was because she was slight and frail. The steward, the bailiff, and the reeve always set her difficult tasks. More often than not they made her work alone. But though she worked as hard as she could, she received little thanks."

To my surprise there was a relief in speaking. How strange it was to have someone listen to me.

I went on: "Sometimes she would hold me to her. At other times she seemed to find me . . . repulsive. Sometimes I thought I was the cause of her misery."

"And your father?"

"He died before I was born. In the pestilence."

"No other kin?"

"None."

His eyes narrowed. "How can that be?"

I shrugged. "My mother said they also died in the Great Death."

"A common enough story. I escaped it."

"How?"

"By running as far north as I could go, to Scotland's wild northern isles. Had your mother no surname?"

"I never knew it."

"Do you ever want to know these unknown things? About your name? Your mother? Your father?"

"I do," I said, "but I don't know how."

He was quiet for a while, as if thinking on what I said. Then he said, "Now, Crispin, tell me of how you came to be proclaimed a wolf's head."

24

Y THEN I HAD SLIPPED SO easily into talking I simply told him what had happened, as much as I could recall.

When I had done he asked, "And they proclaimed you a wolf's head for *that*?"

I nodded.

"To be a wolf's head is to say you're no longer human. So anyone may kill you." He grinned. "Even me. But," he went on seriously, "your priest told you to flee."

"Yes."

"And since your steward tried to kill you, your priest was proved right."

After a moment, I said, "And they killed Father Quinel."

Bear sat bolt upright. "Killed the priest?" he cried. "In the sacred name of Jesus, why?"

"I don't know. But when he told me I had to leave, he also promised he'd tell me something of importance just before I left. Instead, he was slain."

"Have you any idea what he was to say?"

"Something about my father. And mother. So I think his death was my doing. God was punishing me."

"By killing His priest? It's a thing I've noticed," the big man said with laughing scorn, "that the greater a man's—or boy's—ignorance of the world, the more certain he is that he sits in the center of that world."

I hung my head.

"Crispin," he said after a moment of silence, "I'll give you some advice. You're full of sadness. Those who bring remorse are shunned. Do you know why?"

I shook my head.

"Because sorrow is the common fate of man. Who then would want more? But wit and laughter, Crispin, why, no one ever has enough. When I think on the perfections of our Savior, I choose to think most upon His most perfect laughter. It must have been the kind that makes us laugh, too. For mirth is the coin that brings a welcome. Lose your sorrows, and you'll find your freedom."

I remembered the word—*freedom*—as one which Father Quinel used.

After a moment I said, "But you gave me no choice but to stay with you."

His eyes flashed with anger, enough so that I regretted I had spoken. But then, as happened so often with him, he laughed. "Crispin, do you know why my hat is split into two parts?"

"No."

"Like all men with a skill, I wear the livery of my trade. For me, the two-part hat informs the world that there's more than a simple nature residing in my soul. There's bad *and* good."

But I am only bad, I thought to myself, wishing yet again I knew what sin was imbedded in me to have brought God's hand so hard upon me.

"Crispin," said Bear, "a wise man—he was a jester by trade—once told me that living by answers is a form of death. It's only questions that keep you living. What think you of that?"

"I don't know," I said.

"Think on it. For we shall soon be passing out of this zone of desolation. From here on, as God is good, many living villages shall appear. They'll be small, but if we labor well, we can survive, you and I. Will you join me? I give you the freedom to choose."

"You're my master," I said. "I have no choice."

"Crispin, decide," he barked.

I shook my head. "It's not for me to do so."

"Should not every man be master of himself?" he asked.

"You made me call you master."

His face grew redder than it normally was. "You're a willful fool," he bellowed. Clearly frustrated, he poked the fire. "You'll go."

"As you command," I said.

He frowned but only said, "Before we get there, you'll need to learn some things."

"What?"

"Time enough for that tomorrow. Go to sleep." Without further ado, he lay down.

From the pouch around my neck, I took out my cross of lead, and upon my knees, prepared to pray.

"What are you doing?" I heard him ask.

I looked over my shoulder. "Praying."

"What's that in your hand?"

"A cross of lead. It was my mother's," I said, holding it out for him to see. "It even has writing on it."

"Writing or not, it's useless," he said, waving my hand away. "No more than a trinket."

"What do you mean?" I cried, fearing he was slipping back into madness.

"All these things . . . your cross, your prayers. As God is near—and surely He always is—He needs no special words or objects to approach Him."

"But this cross—" I began.

He cut me off. "I know what it is. It's made of lead. Made in countless numbers during the Great Death. Never blessed, they were given to the dying as false comfort. They're as common as the leaves and just as sacred.

"Crispin, as Jesus is my witness, churches, priests—they're all unneeded. The only cross you need is the one in your heart."

Greatly shocked, I didn't know what to say.

"But," he added, with a hard edge of anger, "if you so much as spoke my words in public, do you know what would happen to you?"

"No."

"You'd be burned alive. So don't repeat them. And if you said *I* spoke them, I'd denounce you for a liar and a heretic.

"So, put your cross away. I don't wish to see it again. Keep your faith to yourself."

Though unsettled by his words, I turned away and made my prayers, the cross in my hands.

I prayed to Saint Giles and asked him to remember my father whom I had never seen, my mother whom I missed so deeply, and last of all, myself. I also promised him I'd not believe the things Bear had said.

Though Bear must have heard me, he did not interfere. When I was done, I said, "Bear, I'm sorry I know so little."

"Sometimes it's better not to know."

"How can that be?"

"Ah, Crispin, if I have learned one thing it's that he who knows a bit of everything, knows nothing. But he who knows a little bit well, knows much of all."

He said no more and was soon asleep, grunting like a pig.

The fire had collapsed into a heap of smoldering coals. The night being cold, I drew closer to it and tried to make sense of the things that Bear had said. He had confused me. First he said it was better to live by questions. Then he said it was a mistake to know everything. I struggled to put the two notions together, but could not.

What I did know was that he was unlike any man I had ever known. There was madness in him, to be sure. Yet, I could not deny, some kindness too. . . .

But what vexed me most was his saying that every man should be master of himself. If I knew anything it was that *all* men belonged to someone. Surely God Himself put us all in our places: Lords to rule and fight. Clergy to pray. All the rest—like me—were on earth to labor, to serve our masters and our God.

Otherwise, it was as much to say stars could go their own way instead of being fixed to turn around our world.

Bear had to be wrong. Yet I found myself thinking it was not so bad to have fallen in with him. To be sure, he was a rough-and-ready man. The things he said confused me. Even his calling me by the name *Crispin* was unsettling.

Still, if Bear fed me and protected me, I might, at least, survive awhile. In any case I had little choice. God had willed it.

And yet—thinking on what he said—I asked myself if I *were* to live by questions, what questions would they be? About my father? And those things Father Quinel had said about my mother—if they be true or not. And maybe—I allowed—I'd ask what was to be *my* fate.

25

HEN I WOKE IN THE MORNING, I had spent so much time with Bear's strange ideas I was in a cross mood, not wishing to deal with him. None the less, he informed me that it was time to begin teaching me some skills.

He explained how upon entering a town he played and danced, heading straight for the village church. "There I pray, hopefully at a Mass."

I said, "I thought you didn't believe in such things."

"What I *think*, Crispin, stays in my head. What I *do* is there for all the world to see. I must show reverence."

"I don't understand you!" I burst out, surprising even myself. "You tell me I don't need a church. Then you talk like a priest. What are you?"

"A man. Nothing more or less. And you?"

"Nothing."

"Why do you insist on that?"

"Because I have no name," I said, my rage bursting forth. "No home, no kin, no place in this world. I'm a wolf's head. Any and all may kill me when they choose. Even you. You say you want me to do things. Think things. But when I won't be able to, you'll shun or betray me like the rest."

I had never said so many words in one breath in all my life. When I'd done I turned away, alarmed that I had spoken to my master in such a fashion.

"Crispin, in the name of all the blessed saints, have you ever desired to be anything different from what you are?"

"We must be content to be as God made us," I said.

"What if God wishes you to better yourself?"

"Then *He* will do so."

"Crispin," he said, grabbing me by the neck and hauling me along. "Come with me."

He dragged me to a little stream where we had fetched our water. "Have you ever seen what you look like?" he said.

"A little, by our river. But I don't like to."

"Gaze upon yourself," he said.

Puzzled, I did as he bid, staring at my image in the flowing water: my long hair, my dirty, bruised, and tear-streaked face, my red-rimmed eyes.

"Now, then," he commanded, "wash your face, using sand to scrub it. Go on. Or by God, I'll do it for you."

After I did as he told me, he picked up his dagger.

"What are you going to do?" I cried.

"Cut your hair."

"Now look at yourself again," he said when he was done. "What do you see now?"

I considered my reflection anew.

"Are you different?" he said.

"A little," I said.

"And that was only water and a blade. Think what you might become if you were cleansed of thirteen years of dirt, neglect, and servitude."

I turned back to my image and gazed. It was different. For a moment I allowed myself to wonder what it would be like to alter the rest of myself as well.

"As I was trying to tell you," Bear said, interrupting my thoughts, "when I reach a village, I apply to the priest, to the local lord, or bailiff. The reeve if necessary. Anyone in authority from whom I can get permission to perform."

"And . . . you wish me to go with you?" I asked.

"Of course."

"But, Bear," I said, "what if I'm recognized?"

"Crispin, you are altered. Who would recognize you now?"

"Anyone from Stromford."

"By the certainty of Saint Paul, they are gone. They'll never bother you again."

"But what if they *do*?"

"First you say you are nothing. Then you say half the world is looking for you. Make up your mind. If you have one."

"But, Bear," I said, "the steward tried to kill me. Twice. And when I was hiding in the woods, he came along the road. I'm sure he was searching for me."

He looked at me slyly. "For an insignificant

creature, you're very vain. Give me one reason for their concern."

"They think I'm a thief."

"Crispin, did you steal?"

"As God is my witness, no."

"Then it's all a sham. You were only being blamed for what someone else did."

"But it's they who matter, not me."

"Then I shall make you matter," he said. "I'll teach you music."

"I won't be able to learn," I said.

"Do the birds sing?" he asked.

"Yes," I said.

"Do they have souls?"

"I don't think so," I said, somewhat confused.

"Then surely you can sing no less than they for you have a soul."

"Sometimes . . . I think I have none."

For once Bear was speechless. "In the name of Saint Remigius, why?"

"I have . . . I have never felt it."

Bear gazed at me in silence. "Then we," he said gruffly, "shall need to make sure you do."

26

E BEGAN BY INSTRUCTING me about the pipe's holes—the stops, he called them—and the way to shape my mouth around the blowing end, how to shift my fingers, how to make different sounds.

Reluctantly, I took up the recorder, and with fingers like soft clay, tried to play. What came out were sorry, shallow squeaks. "You see," I said, "I can't do it." I offered him back his pipe.

Refusing, he railed at the top of his voice, threatening to inflict upon me every kind of grisly torture if I didn't try.

At first his shouted warnings terrified me. But as the day wore on, I realized he was mostly bluster. While I didn't doubt he could have done the ghastly acts he threatened, it was but a rough kindness.

The more I realized this, the less tense I became. Gradually I found my way with tongue, fingers, and breath. Before the day was half done, I managed to pipe out his simple song.

"There. You've done it," he cried out when first I did. "Tell me that you didn't hear it, too."

No one was more amazed than me. To think that I, with my breath, could make a song, thrilled me deeply. I wanted to play it over and over again.

Bear only made me work harder. Then, as I played, he began to strike his drum so as to keep the proper beats.

It was midafternoon and I was playing, when something different happened. Before my astonished eyes, this enormous man jumped up and began to dance. Holding his large hands up, pumping his knees high, prancing, his great red beard flapping, his two-pointed hat bobbing this way and that, the hat bells jingling, he was like one possessed. Though a giant, he appeared as light as a goose feather in a swelling breeze.

I was so taken aback at the sight I stopped playing.

"Now you know why I took you on," he said with a grin.

It took a moment for me to fully grasp his meaning—he wanted *me* to help *him*.

"Play, fool," he yelled. "That's the point of it all."

Excited, I resumed, continuing to make music while he paused to scoop up his leather balls. For now, as he danced, he also juggled. Then to all of this he added singing.

"Lady Fortune is friend and foe.
Of poor she makes rich and rich
poor also.
Turns misery to prosperity
And wellness unto woe.
So let no man trust this lady
Who turns her wheel ever so!"

Finally, he stopped.

Panting, he thumped me on the back and said, "There, Crispin, my young and foolish, soulless saint, you see what we shall do. While I perform my revels, you shall pipe the tune. I promise, it shall bring us pennies of plenty and we—the Bear and his cub—shall prosper greatly!"

His words made me grin.

At this Bear thrust his hand aloft, "O God," he cried. "Look upon Thy miraculous gift. This wretched boy has given the world a smile!"

That night, as we made ready to sleep, Bear informed me that on the following day we would reach a village by the name of Burley. "It's only two leagues from where we are. An easy walk," he said. "And on the main road to Great Wexly."

Bear's news about the morrow made me very nervous. Since I had left Stromford, the only person I had been with was him. But I said nothing. He would, I feared, only mock my worries.

Instead, when Bear was asleep, I went upon my knees and with my lead cross in hands, prayed.

"Blessed Saint Giles," I whispered to the cross, "let me play the music well. Let me be a credit to my master. And I beg Thee, let me have a soul, that I too may sing and dance like Bear. And, Saint Giles, do not let him betray me."

27

EXT MORNING WE SET OFF at dawn and soon were trudging along the dirt road. At that place it meandered among low hills, so that we never had a clear view for very far. Only through the tree breaks did we catch glimpses of open fields.

We had been going a little while when Bear abruptly halted.

"What's the matter?" I said.

"Look," he said, pointing to the sky.

I saw nothing but a flock of wood pigeons swirling high above some ways beyond where we were.

"The pigeons?" I said.

"They're agitated by something."

"What?"

"We'd best find out," he said. "Stay close." Straight away he loped off the road, and I followed. He led me into a small spinney, ample enough to hide us from view. Once there, he spied out. Without speaking, he pointed toward a hill some ways across the nearest field. When I nodded my understanding he ran toward it. I kept close.

Upon reaching the base of the hill, he dropped upon his hands and knees. Motioning that I should leave the sack behind, he began to crawl toward the hill crest.

When he reached it, he pulled off his cap, then lifted his head just above the summit. After gazing awhile, he turned slightly, beckoned me closer, and whispered, "Look, but be careful not to show yourself."

Cautiously, I raised my head.

What I saw before me was the road we'd been traveling on, but somewhat farther along. At a place that had been hidden from our view was a small plank bridge spanning a river. Some twelve men were loitering about. A few were sitting on the ground. Others stood by the bridge. All were armed with swords and longbows. It was as if they were waiting for someone.

Among them was one I recognized.

"Bear," I whispered, my heart pounding. "It's John Aycliffe. The steward of Stromford Village."

Bear looked at me—but in a different way than he had before—then at the men again. After a few more moments he edged back. Pulling at my arm, he bade me follow.

We went partway down the hill to a place where we would not be seen. Once there he sat in silence while I waited anxiously for him to tell me what to do.

"Crispin," he said with the utmost solemnity, "mortal men are never perfect. In my life, I've done things I'm ashamed of, things that the all-seeing God shall see emblazoned on my soul. You said they proclaimed you a wolf's head because you stole. You deny you were a thief.

It's not for me to punish you. God awaits. But I must know the absolute truth: by all that's sacred, did or did you not do what they said you did?"

The way he spoke distressed me. Even so, I only said, "No."

He sighed and shook his head. "I believe you. But it makes no sense. They should be glad you fled. At best, you're a nuisance. Why are they searching so hard for you?" he wondered out loud. "And why should they think—or care—that you're heading for Great Wexly?"

"How do they even know?"

"This is the only road," he explained. "Have you anything to say to this?"

"I told you they would come after me."

"You were right. I should have listened more. But, Crispin, there must be something more here, more than you know."

Whatever satisfaction I had in hearing him admit that I was right, paled when I saw his alarm. "What are we going to do?" I said.

"We'll go no farther along this road," he said. "That's certain. But I must go forward. We'd better strike across there," he said, pointing beyond the fields toward some outlying woods. "It'll take us away from those men—and your steward."

Without further ado he rose and marched off with great strides. I rushed to keep up, more than once looking back.

As we went along, I kept thinking how Bear had noticed the birds, which allowed him to see the soldiers. If, I told myself, I was to stay alive in this new world, I must learn such skills as he had. The sooner I learned, I told myself, the longer my life.

28

OR THE REST OF THE DAY we made our way without the benefit of roads. A few times we came upon narrow paths, and these we followed, but only for short times. Instead, Bear went this way, now that, following no reason that I could grasp, other than we moved farther and farther from the steward. As we went he hardly spoke.

"Do you know where you're going?" I finally said.

"To where you can remain alive," he replied.

It was dusk when he finally allowed us to stop. Rain had begun to fall. The dismal drizzle caused the overhanging leaves to drip with irritating monotony. Before a low and flaring fire, which sputtered in the damp, we ate two small pigeons Bear had managed to snare.

Perhaps to shift my mind from my worries, he showed me how he did his snaring, using a few long strands of horsetail hair that he kept in his bag. After tying the strands together he made them into a loop, which enabled him to trap—with great cunning—the birds, without their even knowing they were in danger. I was much engaged.

After eating we stayed on opposite sides of the fire taking what warmth we could. Bear was in a solemn mood and spoke very little, seemingly preoccupied with his own thoughts.

"Do you believe me now?" I said.

"About what?"

"That they are looking for me."

"Yes," he said.

I lay back and recalled what had happened in the forest at Stromford. "Bear," I said, sitting up, "I remembered something else."

"What?"

"The man the steward met had a horse, a fine one. He must have been a man of wealth."

Bear only shrugged.

Then I said, "I wish I knew what the document was that the stranger brought to John Aycliffe. Though, even if I had seen it, I couldn't have read it."

"By and by I'll teach you," he said.

"Bear?"

"Yes, lad?" he said sleepily.

"I've remembered something else. Before I left, the priest told me my mother could read and write."

"How could a miserable peasant woman acquire such skills?"

"I don't know. I never saw her do so. But Father Quinel insisted it was true."

"Did he teach her?"

"He didn't say. But he insisted it was she who wrote on my cross."

Bear rubbed his face and beard, then rolled down onto his back. "Enough," he said. "We'd best sleep. If we intend to survive, we'll need to find a village soon."

As usual, before I lay down I fetched the cross from

the pouch from around my neck and placed it between my hands when I, upon my knees, began to pray.

"Crispin!" I heard Bear cry out.

I looked around.

"Give me that cross."

Remembering what he had said about crosses, and concerned that he might do it some harm, I said, "I'd rather not."

"Give it!" he roared.

"It's precious to me," I said, holding it back.

"By God's honest heart," he said, "I won't do it any harm."

"Do you truly vow?"

"By the bloody hands of Christ," he said.

Though reluctant, I gave him what he wanted. Taking the cross in his great hands—where it seemed even smaller than it was—he peered at it with his shrewd eyes, even feeling it with his fingers. Next he brought it near to the fire.

Knowing that lead could melt in fire, I cried, "Don't cast it away."

Paying me no mind, he held the cross in his palm, in such a way that it was illuminated by our little fire while he squinted at it closely. I realized then that he was looking at the words.

"Can you read what it says?" I asked.

He did not reply. Instead, he handed the cross back to me.

"The light is too weak," he said. "And I need my sleep." With that he rolled onto his back again and closed his eyes.

I looked at him and at the cross, certain he'd found a meaning which he was not prepared to tell.

29

N THE MORNING BEAR WAS much subdued. Now and again, as we prepared to go, I caught him glancing at me when he thought I would not notice. He said nothing, however, and I decided not to ask. I knew him well enough by then that he'd speak only when he chose.

We set off over hills and through woods, until at last we came upon a narrow, winding path. Here Bear paused.

"We'll go this way," he announced. "It will lead us somewhere."

Sure enough, by midmorning we heard the distant tolling of a bell. We stopped.

"There must be a village a league or so ahead," Bear cautioned. "Can you remember everything I told you about how we should enter such a place?"

"I think so."

"Try your tunes," he said.

I took out the recorder and played. He listened intently.

"Good," he said. "You've learned well enough. We'll prosper as long as you do as I've taught you."

Rare for him, he seemed nervous.

"What's the matter?" I asked.

"Crispin," he said solemnly, "if there is any trouble—ever—you're not to pay any mind to me. Just run."

"Run?" I said, taken aback. "From what?"

"If any one should try to harm or apprehend you."

"But where would I go?"

He thought for a moment. "As far north as you can go."

"Why there?"

"You'll be safest out of the kingdom."

"But aren't we going to Great Wexly?"

"We are. On the twenty-third of June, the eve of the Feast of the Saint John the Baptist."

"Why then?" I asked.

"It's Midsummer Day. The city will be crowded with a large market and festivities. That's always good for mummers. We should do well. And, as I told you I have some matters with a man."

"What man?"

He ruffled his beard. "It's a private matter." Then he added as if to mollify me, "I've promised to be there, and so I must."

He was being evasive again, as when I'd asked him about the writing on my cross. "There's more, isn't there?"

"Crispin, I'm part of a . . . brotherhood. It's to make things better. To bring some change."

"Nothing really changes," I said, thinking he had misspoken.

He looked at me with a smile. "Have you not changed?"

"A little," I admitted.

"Crispin, I merely wish to bring some of that freedom you seek." He studied the sky as if some answer might be there. "But I fear the time isn't ready."

"You expect some hazard, don't you?"

Though I knew he heard my question, he acted as if he hadn't. "*Is* there some danger there for me?" I pressed.

"By Saint Pancras," he said, "I was surprised when we saw that gathering waiting for you at the bridge."

"That's for me. What about you?"

He shrugged. "I never fear for myself."

"Why?"

"I make my own choices."

"Then do you fear for me there?"

"Perhaps."

"Why?"

"Crispin, when it comes to the affairs of men, I only worry about what I cannot understand."

"And?"

"I can't make sense of your . . . innocence. In a ruthless world I find innocence more a puzzle than evil."

"Must we go there, then?"

"Crispin, I told you, I promised this . . . brotherhood

that in my travels I'd survey the kingdom. That I would bring them the judgment of my observations. I try to keep my word. They're waiting for me." He picked up some dirt and rubbed it between his hands. "I must give them the benefit of my judgment. That's all."

"You read the writing on my cross," I said. "What did it say?"

He offered up a wry smile. "Crispin, if we wish to survive, it's time for us to go to work."

"Bear—"

"Enough," he said with sudden authority, and turned away.

30

T WAS NOT LONG BEFORE we approached the wooded outskirts of a little village. Its name was Lodgecot, as we would later learn.

When we came out from the trees we saw cultivated fields. Men, women, and children were hard at work—just as at Stromford—plowing, weeding, and hoeing. The clothes they wore could have come right from my home, too. Here and there sheep and cattle grazed. I found it a marvel that I could see so much of the world, yet find it much the same.

As we passed the fields, people paused in their work to look at us. At first Bear ignored them. Only when we drew closer to the village itself did he pause and scrutinize what lay ahead.

"I don't see any signs of trouble," he said.

I looked around. "What kind of trouble?" I asked.

"The people looking for you. Now, play."

Though nervous, I put the pipe to my mouth and began to make music. Even as I did, Bear began his dance. So it was that we entered the village.

If the village of Lodgecot had been exchanged with Stromford, I don't think the world would have noticed. It contained the same cluster of small dwellings along a single rough road with but one or two structures larger than the rest. Every house was roofed with thatch, with walls of wattle and daub. A stone church with a stubby tower stood close to the village center. On a low hill, not far away, I spied a manor house. It was larger than the other houses, but not by very much.

As we came into the village proper, dogs, pigs, and children approached us with a snuffling curiosity. They made sure to keep their distance. It was harder to say who was dirtier, the children or the beasts.

Women emerged from cottages to stare at us guardedly, keeping their younger children behind their skirts. One of these women had a whispered exchange with a child, who promptly raced off toward the church.

Remembering what I'd been told, I, still playing music, headed straight for the church, too. Even as we approached it, a priest emerged, no doubt alerted by the child. He was a younger man than Father Quinel, short, thin, with large round eyes and the stubble of an ill-shaved beard. He did not appear very clean. His robes were quite soiled. Frowning, he stood before the church doors, hands clasped before him.

I stepped aside and let Bear approach. He danced right up to where the priest stood, and then, to my astonishment, halted and sank to his knees, pulling off his cap.

I stopped playing, and hoped my unease did not show.

"Most reverend Father," Bear said in voice loud enough so all onlookers might hear, "I, known as the Bear, am a juggler. My son and I have made our way from the City of York, going toward Canterbury to perform sacred penance. We do humbly beseech your blessing."

The priest visibly softened.

"My boy and I beg your gracious permission to perform some simple songs and dance for the greater glory of God, for this village, and for his grace, King Edward, England's warrior king, with whom I had the honor of fighting on the victorious fields of France."

Then Bear bowed his head, but tilted it somewhat sideways, so as to keep an eye on me. I think he even winked.

The priest looked at Bear, then at me, then at Bear again.

"Do you know sacred songs?"

"I do," said Bear. Hands clapped together in prayer, he began to sing:

"Mary, maiden, gracious and free
Vessel of the Trinity,
Who graciously listens unto me
As I greet Thee with my song
Though my feet unclean be
And my hopes remain unborn.

"Thou art the Queen of Paradise,

Of Heaven, of earth, and all that is.

Thou gave birth to the King of bliss

Without a sin or sore,

Putting to rights all who are poor

Winning life for us evermore."

At the conclusion of his song, Bear bowed his head, crossed himself, and clasped his hands over his chest—the image of humility.

The priest was clearly pleased. Smiling, he raised his hands over Bear's head and pronounced a blessing.

At this, Bear jumped up, and nodded to me. I took it to be a signal to resume my playing, which I did with gusto.

It was not long before most of the townspeople had gathered around us in a great circle. Off to one side, I played the music, while Bear performed in the center. Midway through his dance, he gathered up his leather balls and began to juggle.

I could hear "oohs" and "aahs" from the crowd, as Bear added first a third ball, then a fourth. Then, when he stepped forward and snatched a mazer from the hands of one of the onlookers and added it to the revolving mix, there was laughter and applause.

The young man from whom he'd taken the mazer was a small, one-eyed youth—he wore a patch over his other eye. He also had a thin, scraggly beard that seemed designed to proclaim him older than he was. Though others roared at Bear's antics, this young man took offense at Bear's gambols and, with growing anger, made three attempts to snatch his mazer back.

Each time, Bear, with great dexterity, seemed to offer him the mazer, but at the last moment, tossed it high. This was done to the great hilarity of the crowd, but to the increasing resentment of the young man.

Finally, muttering curses under his breath, the young man stormed away. No one seemed to care.

Attentive to what I'd been taught, I approached Bear. Still dancing and juggling, he inclined his head to allow me to remove his cap. I took it. Holding it before me, I moved about, saying nothing, but begging for coins.

To my great delight, we received a few pennies, as well as some bread.

When Bear was finally done and stood all in a

sweat, people gathered around him, even as children surrounded me and pelted me with questions.

"What's your name?" "Where are you from?" "Where are you going?" "How'd you learn such things?" "Is your father the biggest man in the world?" were among the questions I was asked.

I started to respond honestly, but caught myself and gave another name. Another place. As for Bear, remembering what he had said, I claimed him for my father.

At length Bear called me to his side. Led by the priest—who was nothing but smiles now—we entered the church. Many from the village followed us inside. One of them, I noticed, was the one-eyed young man, who had returned. He gazed at Bear with such malevolence I thought he might offer harm.

The church was like my own at Stromford, though with different imagery on the walls. In particular, there was a vision of Jesus harrowing Hell, the demons frightening to behold.

Before the altar both Bear and I knelt and I, at least, prayed.

"And where will you be going next?" the priest asked afterward.

The onlookers seemed as interested in our answers as was the priest.

"To Great Wexly for the fair on the Feast of John the Baptist," Bear returned, "but always toward Canterbury," he added.

"There are many villages here about," the priest informed us. "But you need to be on the alert for a notorious murderer."

I had been gazing at the images on the walls. Now I turned to listen.

"What do you mean?" Bear said to the priest.

"At a village north of here, I'm not sure which, a boy went mad. After robbing the manor house, he killed a priest."

I hastily looked down lest I give myself away. But as I shifted, I became aware that the one-eyed young man was staring right at me.

"God mend all," Bear cried with horror, making the sign of the cross. "Can't they find him?"

"No one knows where he's fled," the priest said. "But an official came here, along with a troop of armed men. They say the youth is very dangerous. He's been declared a wolf's head. There's a twenty-shilling reward for his taking dead or alive."

"I'm grateful for your warning," Bear said, stony faced. "We would love to earn that money. Who is your lord here?"

"Lord Furnival," the priest replied. "And though he's been gone for these fourteen years, we've received word that—give thanks to God—though gravely ill, he's at last returned to England. We pray daily that he may recover and that we may see him soon."

"God is kind to those who love Him," Bear said. "How did you learn this news?"

"He sent a courier, a man named du Brey."

With many gracious words, Bear took leave of the priest. Then he mingled with the townspeople and asked them many questions, about their crops, their harvests, the life they led.

And though I wished desperately to speak to him, I kept away.

31

HAT AFTERNOON, WHEN WE left the town, Bear told me to play. So it was that we departed the village as we entered, I playing music while Bear danced. This time we were followed by a host of gleeful children.

Gradually, the children abandoned us. It was only when we were entirely alone that Bear ended his dancing. Then I stopped my playing, too.

"Did you hear?" I blurted out right away. "They're accusing me of murdering Father Quinel."

"I heard."

"That priest also said Lord Furnival was their master. How can that be?"

"These lords of the realm own more land than God Himself. Now we need to hurry."

"But when the priest named the courier that had come to them, I recognized the name."

"Did you?"

"It was the man my village's steward, John Aycliffe, met in the woods. Father Quinel spoke his name. And that young one-eyed man you teased, the one who grew angry—I've been trying to notice things—he was paying close attention to me."

Bear shrugged. "We're strangers. For some, strangers are threats, and they look at us accordingly. Pay it no mind."

"But you told them we were going to Great Wexly."

"A small slip."

"Bear . . ."

"What?"

"You also called me your son."

"Ah, Crispin, you could do worse. Far worse." Usually such a remark came with a laugh. This time he was very serious.

"How did I do?" I said.

"Very well."

My heart swelled.

"Shouldn't we be worried?"

"Crispin, there's an old soldier's saying: 'If you have to choose between alertness and worry, being alert will bring you more days of life.' Now, even more important, let us see what we earned."

I had completely forgotten about that. Kneeling on

the ground, Bear emptied his sack. We had earned four silver pennies, four farthings, and six loaves of bread.

"That's so much," I said.

"I'm not so impressed," he said. "But consider, Crispin, it belongs to no one else but ourselves. Honest pay for honest work. And you deserve some too." He offered me a whole penny.

"But I'm your servant," I said.

"Ah, but you have earned it," he said, folding my fingers over the coin. "And we're free men."

I looked at the coin as it lay in my palm. "Are you sure?"

"Did you work hard?"

"I tried."

"Then you deserve it. Now come, we need to earn some more."

We started off again, my thoughts enraptured by the notions that we were indeed free. Then, when I reminded myself that I was still a wolf's head and pursued, the luster of the moment dimmed.

32

VER THE NEXT TWENTY DAYS we sometimes followed roads, sometimes only paths. Now and again we made our way through open fields and woods. Bear did not wish to go in any straightforward way.

During that time we performed in many villages. Each performance was much like the first, though Bear said I grew better, even suggesting I might have skills. He continued to teach me more melodies, and once, I juggled while he played. What's more, our pennies mounted. Never had I felt so free. Never had I felt such constant joy.

Then one evening, Bear said, "Crispin, what do you know of arms?"

His question startled me. "What do you mean?"

"Weapons. The sword. The dagger. The bow."

"Nothing."

"It's time you learned."

"But . . . why?" I said.

"Since you are still a wolf's head, you might as well have some fangs. It could prove necessary."

It was hard to know what upset me more: the weapon; the handling of it; the idea that I might need it; or that I was in such danger that I'd have no choice but to use it.

But I did practice.

At another time when we were before our evening fire, he set about using needle and thread to mend the holes in his leggings. When he'd done, I asked if I could do as much, and would he teach me how. This he did, with much laughter on his part, and frustration on mine.

Once I asked him how he had learned to speak so boldly, not merely to strangers, but even to those above his station.

"It's all in the eyes," he said.

"What do you mean?"

"In faith, Crispin, you have a servile look. When you first came upon me, you kept your eyes upon the ground as if that was where you belonged."

"Where should I look?"

"I've heard it said that a man's soul may be observed behind the eyes."

"Is that true?"

"Perhaps. All I know is that, when I look upon a

man, if he refuses to look at me, I can't see his soul. I'll consider him without and act accordingly. Therefore you need to let people see what lies within you."

"I don't know if I can."

"You doubted you could make music, too."

"Then, from now, when I speak to you," I said, "call 'Eyes!' if I look away or down."

He laughed loudly. "I promise." And so he did.

Then there was the day when I asked him to teach me how to make the snares he used to catch rabbits and birds.

"Do I not catch enough?" he asked.

"The only reason you caught me in that abandoned village," I said, "was because I had no food. What if I'm alone again?"

He looked at me curiously. "You're right," he said with a rueful smile, and commenced to teach me that as well.

At two places where we performed, we learned more of the search for me. Though we discovered nothing new, it meant that they were still looking.

One night, just before he lay back to sleep, Bear said, "Crispin, tomorrow we'll enter Great Wexly."

"What will happen there?" I said.

"Only God in his Heaven knows," he replied. "But," he added, "if you pray tonight, Crispin, pray that the Devil does not know first."

That put me in mind of the images of the demons in the church at Lodgecot. "Bear," I asked, "what do you think the Devil looks like?"

"I suppose the Devil has as many faces as there are sins. At the moment however, I think of him as Lord Furnival."

"Why him?"

"So much of the land we've passed through—and the misery—belongs to him. He treats his people badly."

"Bear, you . . . you won't betray me . . . will you?"

He gave me an angry look. "How can you even ask?"

"Forgive me," I said. "But . . . it has happened."

"And do you think I will?"

"I . . . don't want it."

Frowning, he considered me for a while. "Crispin," he said, "you must know I care for you. Perhaps you remind me of what I once was. And as the Devil knows all too well, liking goes many leagues with me. True, you're as ignorant as a turnip—or perhaps a cabbage—but you've a heart of oak, small acorn though you are.

"What say you to becoming my apprentice? I'll teach you as much as I know, the juggling, singing, and dance. The music making. I'll be your teacher, not your master. Would you care for that?"

"Very much," I said, barely able to speak.

He extended his great hand to me. I grasped it. "Then it is done," he said. "You are henceforward my true apprentice."

Then he lay down and went to sleep.

I could not.

Though I was excited by Bear's promise, I was very nervous. Should I or should I not trust him?

I fumbled for my cross and was about to pray for guidance, but found myself pausing. I had already asked God for much, and he had given in abundance. Perhaps it was time for *me* to make the decision for myself.

With that thought I put the cross away and took a deep breath. I would trust Bear. The decision would be mine and mine alone. But I would stay alert for all that might yet come.

That decision made, I lay down and stared at the stars until I fell asleep.

33

E SET OUT EARLY THE NEXT day beneath gray skies and scudding clouds. The road was muddy, the air moist and cloying. I was very anxious. Though Bear tried to wear his customary cheerful face, I sensed that there was unease on his part, too. Of this, however, he gave no voice.

At first we traveled, as we usually did, alone. By midday, however, people began to join us on the narrow road. As we drew closer to Great Wexly their numbers increased.

To see so many added to my disquiet. Bear, who had come to know my humors well, worked hard to calm me. "You don't have to worry," he said. "You'll be safe. In the name of Jesus, I'll see to that."

As the road began to widen, it became more and more crowded. Knowing how ignorant I was of everything, Bear tried to explain some of what we passed.

"That one is a pilgrim," he said, pointing to a man walking very slowly, his head down. "Notice his gray robes, as well as the heavy metal cross around his neck.

With his hood up and his eyes cast upon the ground, he's surely reflecting on his many sins. From the look of it he'll probably need to go all the way to Avignon to see the Pope in his French palace or perhaps go as far as Jerusalem."

A closed wagon came by, its wheels rimmed with iron, something I'd never seen before and marveled at. Pulled by large horses, it was surrounded by a group of men armed with glaives. The wagon, Bear assured me, contained, "some rich lady, in search of a wayward husband."

"How do you know?"

"I'm only guessing."

"Could it be a rich man?"

"It could," he said with a laugh. "And he looking for a wayward wife."

There were many peasants with baskets and sacks upon their backs. One woman I saw bore two buckets, each one dangling from a shaft, the shaft balanced on her shoulders. Some folk walked besides their wagons. Others pulled them. Children were equally engaged.

Bear pointed out London, Flemish, and Italian merchants, identifying them by their particular garb or badges. There were also a great variety of priests, nuns, and monks.

One monk wore the black robes of the Benedictine order. A Dominican—"They preach well"—was in white. Still another was in rough brown robes and sandaled feet. "He's a begging friar of the Franciscan rule," Bear said. "They take their sacred vows of poverty to heart. May God always look kindly on him and his kind."

He made me give the friar a penny.

Some officials were, he said, from the county. One or two, on horseback, he claimed had come from the royal court in Westminster, close to London.

"Have you been there?" I asked.

"I have," he said, as if it were a common thing.

There were tradesmen, traders, tinkers, masons, and carpenters, hauling goods of one kind or another.

Bear indicated a doctor, a lawyer, and an apothecary. One man, astride a great horse was, he said, a tax collector. He was closely guarded by armed men. Just to see him made Bear irate.

By the roadside were scores of people crying goods for sale or trade. Their offerings were laid out in stalls, low tables, on pieces of cloth, even on the ground. For the most part they were dressed more poorly than others I had seen.

Once a troop of helmeted soldiers passed us by. They were chanting raucously, pushing people aside as they came. In their hands were long yew bows. Quivers of arrows were on their backs.

Aside from the sheer numbers of people, what struck me most were the many ways people dressed, along with the great variety of colors to their clothing, colors I had never seen before, nor could even name. It was as if rainbows had come to earth, draped themselves on these folk, and paraded along the road. I soon realized it was not just words I had to learn to read, but what people wore as well.

"The town will be crowded," Bear said. "You'll see. People come from great distances." He seemed pleased.

Though all but overwhelmed by what I saw, I was fascinated. To be sure, I stayed close to Bear as he strode forward with his great swagger. When people saw him coming they hastily stepped aside, gazing at him in awe once he went by. It made me feel proud. And safe.

But now the market town of Great Wexly loomed before us, as if it had sprung from the ground. Its brown stone walls were immense, stretching away for as far as I could see.

"Where do those walls go?" I asked, for I had never seen anything so vast.

"They surround the town in a great circle," Bear said.

"Why a circle?"

"To keep all enemies out." Then after a pause he added, "And in."

Above the walls I observed spires—some with crosses—from which hung a host of multicolored pennants tossed and turned by breezes. It may seem odd, but it made me think the town had long hair, and each strand blown by wind was yet another color. I saw many housetops, too. It all seemed immeasurable.

By now the people upon the road had swollen to such great numbers, the press became intense. A constant clamor filled the air. I kept turning about, trying to see and hear the all of it, asking Bear what this or that might be. But he, no longer of a mind to answer my endless questions, strode on silently. I found myself reaching out to touch him, lest I fall behind.

As we drew closer to the walls, people began to squeeze together tightly. I wondered why, until I saw the town's entryway before us. Built into the great wall, it was a deep tunnel that revealed just how thick the walls were.

"The Bishop's Gate," Bear said.

This entryway consisted of two massive black wooden doors, each one studded with iron bolts. The doors had been swung open and pushed back against the walls. Behind them, a portcullis had been raised halfway up, looking like teeth prepared to bite.

Above the entryway was a design with markings on it that looked like a shield. Black cloth was wrapped around it. Bear was gazing at it intently, but when I started to ask him what it meant, I realized he'd shifted his gaze to the gate.

I followed his look. Soldiers, their chests covered with iron plates, were guarding the entryway. Pointed metal helmets were on their heads. Tall glaives were in their hands, swords at their sides, daggers on their hips. Atop the walls were other guards. What's more, the soldiers were allowing only a few people in at a time.

Remembering the men at the bridge, I grew alarmed. "I think," I whispered, my mouth dry, "they're looking for someone."

34

EAR PUT A HAND ON MY shoulder. "Crispin," he said softly, "try to show less worry. The worst disguise is fear."

"What if they stop me?"

"I don't think they will. But if they do, always remember what I told you; run away. Head into a crowd. Your size will hide you."

Watching intensely, I saw that those trying to get into the town had formed two lines which pressed through a gauntlet of soldiers. As we slowly made our way forward, I could feel myself becoming increasingly timorous.

"Here's a better way," Bear said into my ear. "When I tell you to—when we're close to the gate—start playing the pipe. I'll dance."

"But won't that make them pay more attention?" I said.

"Do as I say," he said, but in so tense a fashion I dared not question him.

Instead, we edged along. Just as we approached the gate—and the soldiers—Bear said, "Begin."

I hastily made the sign of the cross over my heart, called on Saint Giles to protect me, and with trembling fingers took up the recorder and began to play. Bear began to beat his drum and dance. People turned to look. There were smiles on their faces, and from some, applause. That included the soldiers.

We fairly well danced our way up to the gate and through the town walls with not so much as an unkind look from anyone.

"Well done," said Bear with a palpable sigh of relief as we entered Great Wexly itself.

If I had been amazed by what I'd seen on the road, I was more astonished once within Great Wexly. For we had hardly passed through the gate, when I saw more people—men, women, and children—in that one moment than I had seen in all my life together. Just the din that burst upon my ears was beyond belief. People were shouting, calling, arguing, laughing, selling their wares to any and all from where they stood. Wandering water carriers were proclaiming what they sold. So were those who offered apples, lavender, or ribbons.

It was hard to know who was talking to whom. It all appeared to my eyes and ears like a flock of crows screaming at one another in a crowded field of new-threshed wheat.

No, it was more like a dense forest, not of trees, but people. For we could not walk straight, but had to weave our way along, constantly bumping, banging into others.

In Stromford Village you could not pass anyone without knowing them and receiving some nod of greeting, perhaps a grunted word or two. Even I received such notice. There, strangers were as rare as shooting stars, and just as portentous. But though Bear and I were strangers to Great Wexly—and I a wolf's head—no one seemed to care, though they did glance at Bear, if only on account of his size.

Still, what assaulted my senses more than anything—aside from the sheer numbers of people of all ages and the ensuing cacophony—was the stench that filled the air: rotting goods, food, dung, manure, human slop, and swill, mixed together into such a ghastly brew as to make me want to swoon.

In my village, refuse was heaved behind our houses. In Great Wexly, foulness lay on the wide road where we walked. This road was no longer dirt and mud, but laid out in stone. A filth-filled gutter—like an open gut—ran down its middle. Even as we passed, I saw house shutters opened and muck heaved out on the street, sometimes dousing passersby, to the hilarity of those watching, arousing fury from the victims.

Nor was it only people I saw, but animals: pigs, chickens, geese, dogs—and rats—all of which scurried among the crowds with as little thought to people as the people seemed to give to them.

Pressing in on the crowded, narrow streets were looming walls of close-built buildings, structures two, sometimes three, stories high, with slate, not thatch, roofs. These houses were, for the most part, built of timber beams with pale mortar filling in between the wood. Here and there stood stone buildings of even grander proportions. Many houses had their upper stories built so that they extended over the narrow streets, blotting out the sky.

The houses had countless windows, mostly with shutters but some with glass, more than I had ever seen before. As for doors, I did not think the world had so many. These people, I thought, must live their lives by little more than entries and exits.

And again, on many places there was black cloth draped with intertwining ribbons of blue and gold. I asked Bear what it meant.

This time he replied, "Someone important has died."

From numerous buildings hung great wooden images of things: a pig here, a helmet there, a fish, a jacket, a hoop, even a sheaf of wheat. These—as I was to discover—were emblems to inform passersby of the nature of the business or goods made or sold therein. Tradesmen simply lowered their shutters onto the streets, making a kind of shelf from which they marketed their goods. As for sleeping and eating, people did that in the second- or third-floor solars.

There was so much to see, I barely looked at one thing but felt compelled to look at yet another. Indeed, there were so many objects to look at that if I had had ten eyes I could not have seen them all. It made my head ache.

More than once Bear had to haul me in, or yell, for, dumbfounded by what I saw, I would halt in my tracks and stand in danger of being knocked down and trampled by the swarming people. For instance, I saw a bakery that sold bread that was swan white, something I had never seen before. And meat. I swear, by Jesus' name, there was more meat than the whole kingdom could consume. I had always known that Stromford Village had little enough to eat, but assumed it was no different from the rest of the world. Now I discovered how poor my village was.

On and on we went, until Bear unexpectedly grabbed me by my arm and swung me around.

"Look," he said.

We were in front of a building from which a straw-stuffed man, painted all in green, dangled from a pole.

"What's that mean?" I asked.

"It's the Green Man tavern. Where my affairs will be conducted."

Bear boldly pushed through the doorway. Though I followed on his heels, I was more than a little hesitant, knowing his business—as he had said himself—was dangerous.

35

E ENTERED INTO A LARGE room in which a few small tallow candles had been stuck into crannies in the walls. Despite the sputtering light, it was a dim and smoky place that reeked of bad ale, stale bread, and sour wine. Trestle tables and benches, more than I had ever seen in one place, stood beneath a low beamed ceiling. The floor was made of thick wood slabs, strewn with dirty rushes. To one side stood a kind of counter, upon which sat rows of wooden tankards.

Behind this counter stood a large, buxom woman. Dressed in a brown, grease-spotted kirtle, she had a lop-sided white linen cap upon her dark and gray-streaked tresses. Around her waist was a belt of glassy rosary beads, from which dangled a leather purse. Wooden pattens were on her feet. As for her face, it was a flushed and rosy red. Her nose was flat, as if it had once been broken. Her cheeks were sunken, too. Withal, she cast off a brimming, bustling force.

When we came forward, she squinted to see who was there. As Bear loomed large before her, a grand grin spread upon her face, revealing not just joy, but a complete lack of teeth.

"God's wounds," she cried with lisping, spittle-spraying laughter, "it's the Bear set loose among us again."

"And on my honor," Bear said, his voice booming, his arms spread wide, "it's the Widow Daventry."

The two embraced in the middle of the room.

"Welcome back to Great Wexly," the woman said, pushing Bear away even as she looked him up and down. "I was wondering if you'd come. But you've been true."

"Fair lady." Bear laughed, making a mock bow. "I always keep my word."

"But once again, sir, I fear you've not come to court me," she said.

"Alas, it's my other business," said he.

Then, to my astonishment, the woman smote him hard in the chest with a tight fist, a blow which only made him laugh even more. Not content with that assault, she pulled his beard and tweaked his cheek. "And what escapades have befallen you since you were here last?" she asked, laughing with such delight I could not keep from grinning too.

"Many an adventure, you can be sure," he said. "And there stands one of them." Bear pointed at me.

The woman turned and considered me with squinty eyes. "Is he yours, or did you find him in some swamp?"

Before he answered, Bear looked around. What he might have been searching for I don't know, for only the three of us were there.

"It was God's sweet grace that let him find me."

"How did that happen?"

"We met in an abandoned village. He had fled his village."

"Did he?" the woman said and looked at me with new interest. "For what reason?"

"In search of a grander world," said Bear.

"And what of his father? His mother?"

"Both gone to a better world."

"An orphan then. And not pursued?" she asked, clearly relishing the tale.

"That's another matter," Bear said with a frown. "But by the laws of this realm," he said, "he's fully bound to me now. My apprentice. And a likely lad."

It felt good to hear his praise.

"What's your name?" she asked me.

I made myself look up. "It's . . . Crispin."

"Now there's a highborn name for a lowly lad," the woman said. "But, Crispin, pay no heed to my bantering. Bear's friends are mine. Welcome to the Green Man's Inn. Where do you come from?"

When I hesitated, Bear said, "Crispin, name your village."

"Stromford," I said.

"Never heard of it," the woman said with a shrug.

"One of Lord Furnival's holdings," Bear said.

"Lord Furnival," the woman said, turning from me back to Bear. "Have you not heard the news?"

"That Lord Furnival died?" he said.

"Aye. Two weeks ago," the woman said.

As Bear made the sign of the cross over his heart, I said, "How did you know?" not sure which surprised me more, that he had known or that he hadn't told me.

"The black cloth draped around town," he replied. "And the extra soldiers at the gates."

"To be sure," the woman said. "When great men die there's always unrest. He died in his bed," she added. "From the wounds he earned at the French wars. I suppose it will only encourage your enterprise," she said with some unease.

"Widow," he said, "it's not *my* enterprise."

As I watched and listened to the two of them, it was clear she had more knowledge of Bear and his business than I. It gave me a jealous pang.

"Who will succeed the lord?" Bear said.

"He has no legal heirs," the woman said. "Though it's been rumored there are some illegitimate ones."

"And all his property?"

"It now belongs to his widow, the Lady Furnival. Unless some bastard son—with an army at his back—makes a claim. Or until she marries. *If* she marries. But they say that's unlikely. She's not the type to relinquish her new powers. She never traveled with Lord Furnival, but preferred to stay in her court. You know what women say," she added with a grin: "'If the first marriage is a gift from God, the second comes straight from Hell.'"

That said, there was an awkward moment of silence. Bear was tense. I did not know exactly what had occurred, but it made me recall something Father Quinel had told me once at confession: a moment of silence in the midst of talk means Death's Angel is close at hand.

I shuddered.

36

UT YOU," SHE SAID TO BEAR, "must sit and slake your thirst. I want to know all you've learned since you've last been here."

Bear relaxed. "If you'll be so good as to fetch me

the key to my room in the solar—the *special* one," he added, "I'll settle the boy. Then we can speak."

Though realizing I was being put aside, I said nothing, but simply followed Bear.

Key in one hand, he led me up the steps to the second story. I had never climbed so high in a building before, so high that I furtively put a hand to the wall to steady myself.

We went along a dark, narrow hallway until we reached a door, which he unlocked.

"Our solar," he informed me. "Go on."

I stepped inside. By the little light that seeped through a shuttered window, I observed a small room. Old rushes lay on the floor. A small, low table stood in one corner. In another corner was a large pallet of hay. The place had a rank, close smell of sweat and ale that made me feel slightly ill, used as I was to open air.

Bear fluffed up the pallet.

"Bear?"

"What?"

"This building . . . it's so high. Might . . . might it fall down?"

He looked at me for a disbelieving moment, then

erupted with one of his big laughs. "There is no chance. None."

There was a knock on the door. Widow Daventry entered. In her hands was a bowl with meat in thick sauce. Pieces of bread were mixed in. To my surprise, she offered it to me. I took it gratefully.

"Yours is below," she said to Bear and left.

I sat on the hay cross-legged, bowl in my lap, horn spoon in hand.

As Bear removed his dagger and laid it on the table, I said, "Will we perform here?" I asked.

"I think not," he said to my further surprise. "Our time here will be very short. But I must show you something." He went to the wall, and felt about the wooden boards. "This is a special room," he said. "My friend below always gives it to me."

Under the pressure of his hands, a slab of wood popped out from the wall. "It's a hiding place. It will hold you, and me too, for that matter, if there's need."

"Will there be a need?"

"By all of Heaven's sacred saints, I pray not."

"Bear," I said looking directly at him, "what is it you *really* do?"

He laughed. "When we met," he said, "you dared not even ask my name. Now you stare brazenly at me and presume to ask of my affairs. Have we risen in the world, or fallen?"

"That's for you to say," I said.

"As to what I *really* do," he said with a placating smile, "I'm a fool because I should like to be in Heaven *before* I die." He reached for the door.

"I don't want to stay here," I said. "It's close and ill smelling."

"You'll do as you're told."

"Yes, master," I said, knowing my saying so would irritate him. "Then at least don't lock the door."

"I won't," he said, then paused. For a moment I thought he would speak more. But all he said was, "Crispin, on your life, remain here until I return." With that, he left.

Feeling much aggrieved, I ate the food, then lay back upon the straw. I was not very happy. Why, I asked myself, should I remain in such a stuffy place while he did as he pleased? Besides, my glimpses of the town had only whetted my curiosity. And I had a penny of my own. There was much still to see, but it sounded as if Bear intended to keep me in the room for what now appeared to be a short stay.

For a while I remained where I was, though as time passed, I fretted more and more.

Finally, I got up, went to the door, and peeked into the hall. Seeing no one about, I made up my mind to wander the town for a short time. My intent was that I would return before Bear even noticed I had left.

I was just about to leave when I went to the table and plucked up Bear's sheathed dagger and hid it underneath my tunic. Had he not taught me to use it? Was not this the town in which to claim my liberties?

Moving quietly, I crept halfway down the stairs and listened. From somewhere I could hear the murmurs of Bear's talk, as well as Widow Daventry's. Exactly where they were I didn't know.

I continued down, until I was certain no one was in the tavern room.

At the base of the steps, I decided it would be better if I didn't use the front door, lest they see me. Instead, I made a sharp turn and went along a narrow hall. At the end of it I reached a small door.

Pushing it open, I stepped into an alley that had

the most appalling stench. It was the place where privies were set over open ditches.

Holding my nose, I shut the door behind me, and raced away.

37

T WAS MIDAFTERNOON, shortly after the bells had rung for None, when I stepped away from the back door of the Green Man. Running, I regained the main street and once there began to look upon the town at my ease.

As I went about, the hurly-burly world of countless people, buildings and wares, struck me with even greater force. If anything, Great Wexly seemed more tumultuous, with more people, more happenings than even before. But I was feeling bold and quite sure of myself. I don't need Bear to see the world, thought I.

As I stood upon the street—enjoying the buffeting of those who passed, not sure which way I wished to go—a crowd of children rushed by, yowling and laughing.

Curious to know where they would go and what they would do, I ran after them.

The young people turned this way and that, and then, just as they had appeared, they vanished. I had not the slightest idea where they had gone.

Though baffled, I was not a bit disconcerted. With so much to see, I was content to ramble on, pausing to look at whatever took my interest, of which there was no scarcity. As for my penny, I purchased some white bread from a street vendor. It was light and sweet, and took little chewing to get down, which I found passing strange.

After a while I found the courage to leave the main, stone-paved street, and began to wander among back ways. These proved to be dirt and mud lanes. Though very narrow, they cast an even greater stench than the main thoroughfare.

These ways twisted and turned in every conceivable direction, with no logic that I could grasp. Yet I found myself excited *not* to know where I was going. How marvelously odd, I thought, to be required to pick and choose which way to go. What did I care that I had to make so many choices? It give my head a pleasing whirl.

And still more people. Of so many kinds. Some I

could see—from the way they dressed—were poor. Yet even so, they appeared to mingle with others of far greater wealth, and no one took offense.

In time I found myself upon the main stone street again. It was there I saw a woman riding sidesaddle astride a great black palfrey whose saddle and harness were trimmed with gleaming silver. Though the lady wore a black cape, I could see her gown. It was a brilliant blue, trimmed with golden fur. Her hair was tucked behind a squared-off, ruffled, netted cap of black lace. Her feet were shod in golden shoes with pointy tips. Her small hands were encrusted with sparkling jewels. As for her face of elder years, it was pale and haughty, and did not—or so it seemed—take in the world about her. Yet as she went by, she pressed a silken cloth to her nose as if to block the offending street stench. Her nose knew where she was.

Before her marched a boy dressed entirely in black, a short gold-and-blue cape draped over one shoulder. He carried a long horn of bright metal from which dangled a flag of blue and gold. With every few steps he took he lifted the horn to his lips and blared out notes to announce the lady's progress.

Clustered around this lady were six men, wearing

tunics with padded chests, their puffed sleeves lengthened to cover half their hands. One man led the lady's horse. Others marched on either side of her, while three more came behind. By the swords they carried, it was clear they were her guards. Though not so sumptuously dressed as she, they were splendid enough to look upon in their blue-and-gold livery. On each left sleeve was a band of black.

For me she was an amazing sight. I had never seen such astounding wealth. Another marvel for my eyes.

As she passed, people on the streets hastily made way for her, some doffing their hats, or inclining their heads in reverence. Some even went down upon their knees, so I knew her to be a personage of great power.

And yet when the noble lady had once gone by, the crowds knitted together just as before, milling about, strolling, buying or selling. It was as if she had never been there.

"Who was that?" I asked a boy standing near.

He gave me a look of astonishment, as if I should have known. "Why, it's Lady Furnival."

I turned quickly to look after her, but she had gone.

38

LL AFTERNOON I WANDERED in a kind of daze, beguiled by what I saw. It was as if my world had multiplied many times in size, numbers, and wealth. My eyes fairly ached with marvels seen even as my heart beat with sheer excitement. As for my anxiety about being in the town, it melted clear away.

And then, at that point in my wanderings, when I thought I'd seen all there was to see, I came upon the town's great square.

Here, in a vast open space—greater than Stromford's entire commons—buildings pressed in on all sides. Some seemed new, some old, some were straight, while others sagged. But the square was dominated by two buildings which stood at opposite sides.

By far the biggest structure was a great church—a cathedral as I would learn—which soared upward with a multitude of towers. These towers, joined together by what looked like floating arches, were emblazoned with countless embellishments and statues that seemed as real as life. Set between the high front towers was a vast circle of stone and multicolored glass. Below it was the main entry, deep-framed with columns and more statues. The whole gigantic structure seemed to rise toward Heaven itself, stone leaping into glory.

Opposite the church, on the other side of the square, was a large stone building some three stories tall. Whereas the church rose high, this building seemed to cling to the earth with a weight and bulk that bespoke earthly power.

On its first level were big wooden doors over which had been set an open space, caged in with metal bars. To either side of these doors were small windows, similarly enclosed. But on the second level—at a considerable height—were four huge windows side by side, with pillars and stone tracery. Set before the windows was a balcony under which stone lions' heads protruded. Flags, with various designs of blue and gold, hung on poles. Others flags were black. Here too, soldiers paced.

The third level had smaller windows. But unlike the church, which stood alone, this building was hemmed in close on either side by ordinary structures.

Between the church and this large building was the great open space—the town square itself. It held crowds of traders with booths and stalls, with more sellers of goods and food than I could count.

Swarms of buyers were in attendance. Most were walking, but a few were on horseback, wending their way through the middle of the crowds.

I walked about the square gazing at the endless numbers of things being sold, many of them objects I'd never beheld before; cloth of many colors and types; Moscovy furs; Toledo daggers; Flemish hats; Italian gloves. There were baskets, boxes, and boots. There were shoes, tools, and armor. As for food and spices, why, I actually saw a bowl full of peppercorns. And everywhere coins clinked and abacuses rattled. I wished I had not already spent my penny.

Timidly, I approached the great church itself. For a while I stood before it, trying to decide if I might be allowed to enter. What, I wondered, might it be like to pray in such a place? But aside from its great size, it was the soldiers about the doors that made me hold back. Yet they seemed to be paying very little attention to the crowds of people who went in and out. When I saw children enter, I made the sign of the cross over my heart and went forward.

In truth, the soldiers barely looked at me as I passed through an entryway crowned by statues of Mary and Jesus, plus other saints whose names I did not know. I promised myself I'd return with Bear, who would, I was certain, know them all.

But when I stepped past the vestibule, I gasped. Before me was a space of such immense size, height, depth, and breadth, that I never would have thought it could exist on mortal earth. Burning candles blossomed everywhere, enough to awe the stars. Through sweet and smoky air, great columns rose to dizzying heights, while enough multicolored light poured down through stained glass so as to turn the hard stone floor into pools of liquid hues. From somewhere unseen a chorus of swelling chant rolled forth, filling this celestial space with sounds that made me think of the measured beating of angels' wings. It was as if I had entered paradise itself.

Any number of people were milling about, or were on their knees in prayer. Afraid to go any farther, I sank to my knees, too, pressed my hands together, and simply stared with wonder at the church itself and then at the people.

As I knelt, my gaze fastened on a particularly

devout man who was kneeling, hands tightly clasped in prayer. Though he was wearing a soldier's quilted canvas jacket, red leggings, and high, leather boots, somehow he seemed familiar. After a while he began to look about.

As he turned, the hairs at the back of my neck began to prickle. In truth, I could hardly believe what I was seeing. It was none other than John Aycliffe, the steward of Stromford Village.

Moreover, I now realized he was not alone, but attended by men dressed in the same livery as those the great lady I had seen had about her person.

Even as I began to grasp who it was, Aycliffe shifted farther about. Before I could gather my wits, he turned full-face toward me.

Our eyes seemed to fasten on one another. It was as if neither of us could believe the other was there, and we were in Stromford's forest once again.

But then he set up a cry, shouting, "There!" and pointed right at me. "The boy! The wolf's head! He's here! Catch him!"

These men, taken by surprise, spun around, saw whom he meant, then began running in my direction, shouting, knocking down anyone who stood in their way.

By then I had collected wits enough to leap to my feet and race out of the church. Once outside, I plunged into the mass of people in the square, pushing and dodging to get away.

After leaving the square, I raced on without any knowledge of where I was, running through one narrow lane after another. I went in no particular direction and never paused to look back. All I could think was that I had to get back to Bear.

How long I ran, I don't know. But I was still pelting through a particularly narrow lane when a man leaped out in front of me.

"Halt!" he cried, his arms spread wide enough to prevent me from passing.

39

ULPING FOR BREATH, I HALTED and spun about, only to find that another man had come up behind me. I flung myself against a wall, even as I struggled to get Bear's dagger out of my pocket.

With the two men keeping to either side of me, I was unable to confront them both. But one, I saw, had a large stick in his hand. The other held a knife.

"Keep away!" I screamed, finally managing to pull Bear's dagger free from its sheath. Though my heart was pounding and my legs were shaking, I held it before me as Bear had taught me.

The dagger caused my attackers to hesitate. In that moment I made a clumsy lunge at the man with the stick. Not only did he nimbly leap out of the way, he brought his stick down hard on my wrist. The pain and shock were so great I dropped the dagger. The next moment arms locked around me from behind.

I kicked, and butted my head back. There was a sharp grunt, and the man's arms went slack, just enough to allow me to break his grasp. Head down, I charged straight at the man with the stick, catching him in the chest. He fell back.

It was enough. With a burst, I ran past him down the alley. Then I plunged along a different narrow way, taking one turn after another, not daring even to glance back to see if I were being followed.

I don't know how long I ran before I stopped and

looked behind. Seeing no one, I allowed myself a moment's rest.

Heart thudding to the point of pain, my wrist still smarting where it had been struck, I tried to grasp what had happened.

Why Stromford's steward was in Great Wexly was something I could make no sense of. But what was clear was that, far from escaping the pursuers who wished me dead, I'd come to a place where they could trap me.

In my frantic state I was quite sure that not even Bear could protect me. What's more, I had disobeyed him. It was not a thing, I was sure, he would forgive. And hadn't he told me to run away if attacked?

I made up my mind to leave the town. I would get beyond the walls and flee. Exactly where I'd go didn't matter, as long as I escaped.

While it was easy to make the decision, I quickly realized I had no idea where I was or where to go in order to leave. With my distress growing every moment, I looked around, trying to get some sense of my whereabouts.

When I had first arrived in Great Wexly, I had been overwhelmed by the multitude of *different* things I saw. Now, in a complete turnabout, my panic made everything seem the *same.* What's more, I couldn't help but feel that lurking behind each corner, each bend of each alley, would be more of my enemies.

Still, I also knew I couldn't remain where I was. My pursuers had already proved they knew the town well enough to track me down.

Moving with great caution, I wandered down one alley after another, spying ahead even as I constantly checked behind. What made things worse was that no matter where I went, I had the sensation I'd been there before. It was as if I could make no progress.

But then I came to what seemed a good idea: Bear had told me that the great walls *encircled* the entire town. If that was the case—and I didn't doubt him—I supposed that I could find some part of them as long as I walked a straight line in any one direction. Then, once I found the walls, I'd follow around until I came to the gate through which we had entered. From there I'd make my exit from the town and flee to safety.

Feeling somewhat less apprehensive now that I had a plan, I immediately set off. Though I hurried, I remained alert lest I blunder into another attack. Again and again I made myself slow down.

Try as I did to follow a straight line, I soon discovered it was impossible. The alleys and streets meandered in ways that bewildered me. It was as if I were in a maze.

Even so, I forced myself to go on because I was afraid to stay in any one place. So I made my way by hugging walls, slipping round corners, all but crawling.

Daylight was fading. The long summer twilight had begun to ebb. With it came a resumption of a chilly rain. Soon, misty dimness cloaked the air. The brightest light came from within houses, or the occasional passerby who made his way holding a flaming rush or lantern before him.

Fewer and fewer people were abroad. Shadows lengthened. Now and again men would stagger by, clearly having had too much to drink. The only other noise—and it came from shuttered houses—was an occasional burst of laughter, an angry shout, a child called.

At last I made out the town walls. They rose high over my head and seemed to melt into the murky sky. Nor were they smooth walls, as I had imagined, but had houses built close against them.

Even so, as far as I was concerned, I was making

progress. Now—according to my plan—I needed only to follow the wall around. If I did, surely I would come upon the gate through which Bear and I had entered the town.

Once again my plan was faulty. The wall had not been built in a simple circle, but was in fact serpentine. Still, I continued on until I stumbled on a wide street paved with stone. When I recognized it as the one on which Bear and I entered the town, I started to run along it.

Then two things happened almost simultaneously: the town's church bells began to ring. And I saw what appeared to be a gate in the wall. Some nine or ten soldiers were milling about it. A few carried flares. Though I wasn't sure if it was the same gate by which Bear and I had entered, I told myself it didn't matter. It was a way out of town.

I ran toward it. Even as I did, the great doors—hauled by soldiers—swung in and shut. Not believing what I was seeing, I stopped, aghast, and watched as the soldiers dropped huge beams across the doors to brace them shut. Then they added chains, and even locks to keep the doors securely closed.

Having shut the gates, most of the soldiers began to stroll away, leaving only two behind.

I drew close enough for them to notice me. "Did you want to leave?" one of them called.

"Yes . . . sir," I said.

"Too late. They're closed. They'll be open in the morning at Prime. Now get yourself away. The curfew has begun. You should be behind doors."

I remained standing where I was, unsure what to do.

"Be off with you," a soldier shouted. I turned and began to wander away.

It had become night. The rain intensified. The streets—now swamps of muck and mud—were all but deserted save for a few laggards. Even they moved hurriedly, no doubt wanting to get behind doors lest they be taken up and charged.

Animals began to emerge—mostly pigs and dogs, but rats, too. They were splashing about in search of things to eat.

As night thickened, people put up their house shutters. The town grew even darker than before.

Hearing the sound of marching, I turned quickly. Some six helmeted soldiers, armed with broadswords and bearing lanterns, were coming down the street.

I leaped into a narrow alley, and peered out.

As they went by, one of the soldiers shouted out, "The hour of Compline is at hand! The curfew is in force! No one may be on the streets!"

As they passed, I shrank back, listening as the tramp and shouts grew fainter.

It was night now. The town seemed asleep. The sky was black. The rain still fell. I wandered on, wet and miserable, looking for a place to conceal myself, hoping I might stumble upon the Green Man. The only sound I heard was the *squish* of my feet on the mud or stones. I hardly dared to breathe.

Then I heard the sound of running feet. I pressed myself against the wall and peeked out around a corner. A group of men, torches held aloft, hurried past. By the light of their torches I glimpsed their blue-and-gold livery. It was the same livery as Lady Furnival's entourage wore. But I recognized them as the steward's men.

How could that be?

Then I recalled something that I had heard the stranger say in the forest: Aycliffe was Lady Furnival's kin.

I wanted to think things through but feared to take the time. Instead, I backed away and scurried down the narrowest of alleys, the walls so close I could have touched either side by stretching out both arms. I was halfway down it when I saw the hulking form of someone lurching toward me, hooded lantern in hand.

I stopped, turned, and began to run in the opposite direction only to hear a thunderous, "Crispin! Stop!"

40

EARING MY NAME CALLED so terrified me, I stopped and turned around. The man had drawn closer, but as I could not see his face, I shrank away.

Only when the voice called out again, even angrier, "Crispin, you stunted son of a scoundrel!" did I realize it was Bear.

Heart exploding with relief, I ran toward him and flung myself at his knees, embracing him with fervor.

"Where, by the sins of Lucifer, have you been?" the huge man said, setting his lantern on the ground. Prying me loose, then putting his great hands on both my shoulders, he made me stand before him. At the same time he went to his knees, so I could look into his eyes.

"Bear . . ." I said, unable to say more because I had put my arms about him and pressed into his neck and beard, like an infant sparrow returned to his nest.

"Crispin," he scolded, "I waited all afternoon for you to return. Did you forget me so soon? Is this the way you repay my kindness? I should give you a sound whipping."

"I didn't mean to. I lost my way. And I was attacked."

"Attacked?" he said, prying me loose from his neck so he could look into my face. "By whom?"

"The steward's men."

"What steward?"

"From Stromford. John Aycliffe. He's come after me," I went on in a rush. "I saw him in the great church. But he saw me too. The moment he did, he set men upon me. And Bear, I remembered something else: he's Lady Furnival's kin. I even saw her. You said Great Wexly was Furnival's principal home. That Stromford was one of his holdings. Now that Lord Furnival is dead, Lady Furnival must have summoned Aycliffe."

"I feared that might happen."

"Why didn't you tell me?"

"I wanted to avoid it all."

"My wrist is numb where they struck me."

"Then you'll have to walk on your feet," he said, grinning.

With that, he turned about, and began to wend his way through back streets and dark alleys, his lantern barely showing the way through the dark and rain.

"When I tried to defend myself," I said after we had gone for a while, "I lost your dagger."

"I'm sure you used it well."

"Bear?" I said as we went along.

"What?"

"God bless you."

"And you also," he returned gruffly.

Only when I was secure behind the doors of Widow Daventry's inn did I draw a fully relaxed breath. I looked about. The main room was deserted.

"Bear, you need to tell me what I should do if—"

The widow came into the room. As she did Bear put up his hand to silence me.

"Ah," the woman said. "You found him."

"He was wandering and became lost," Bear said, not mentioning the attack.

"Did the watch see you?" she asked me.

"I don't think so."

"Good." She drew herself up. "I'm afraid John Ball has just arrived."

"Where is he?" Bear said.

"In the kitchen. He demanded to be fed."

"Fine. I'll get the boy to the room. Can you fetch him something to eat? And some dry clothes."

"I'll get some," the woman said and left the room.

Giving me no explanation as to what his exchange with Widow Daventry had been about, Bear and I returned to our room. Once there, he set the lantern on the table, then bade me lie down on the pallet. When I did, Bear sat down by my side, but instead of speaking became lost in his thoughts. Even so, I felt comforted.

Widow Daventry opened the door and stuck her head inside. "He's getting anxious," she said.

"He always was the impatient man," Bear muttered. "I'm coming."

The woman left. Bear stood and stepped toward the door.

"Now eat your bread and go to sleep."

"Will you truly forgive me?" I said.

"There's nothing to forgive. Sometimes I forget."

"Forget what?"

"How little you know."

With no further words, he went away.

Left alone, I hardly knew what to think. But after what had just happened to me—and how he had come after me—I had no heart to question him.

41

SAT ON THE STRAW AND ATE the bread. Afterward, wanting to give thanks for my safe return, I took Goodwife Peregrine's pouch from around my neck, and removed my mother's cross of lead. With it in my hands, I began to say my prayers in a low voice.

As usual, I prayed for the well-being of my

mother's and my father's souls. This time I added Bear's name to those for whom I begged protection.

Prayers done, I lay back on the pallet and thought of all I had seen and done that day. It was hard to grasp.

Then I listened to the rain as it continued to beat down, hoping it would lull me to sleep. My mind kept returning to this man, this John Ball, whom Bear was meeting, wondering if he were part of my puzzle, and why Bear was hiding him from me.

Unable to resist, I got up and crept out the door, then out to the dim hall. When I reached the steps I moved down silently, holding on to the wall for balance. Halfway, I paused and looked into the dimly lit room.

Bear was sitting at a table, his back to me. Standing by his side was Widow Daventry. Seated opposite was a man, who I assumed was John Ball.

Compared to Bear, the man was quite small, though his face, what I could make out of it, was strong, with a large nose, deep-set eyes, and a severe mouth. His brown robes and tonsured hair showed him to be a priest.

That in itself surprised me, because Bear had told me he had little faith in priests.

". . . and the city apprentices," I heard Bear say, "what of them?"

"Of like minds," said John Ball. "As angry as any other. The constant wars in France, the taxes and harsh fees, these things grind them down as well as any man, peasant or not. They want—need—better wages and an end to the guilds."

"All that may be true," Bear said, "but from what I've seen and heard in my travels, they won't rise up now."

"They will if they can their reclaim their ancient freedoms," said Ball. "And, with the righteous hand of God"—he lifted a fist—"it is my destiny to lead them."

"Then you had better to wait till King Edward dies," Bear said.

"How long will that be?"

"Soon."

"Can you be certain?"

"It's all the talk of London, " Bear said, "as well as the court at Westminster."

"And who will succeed to the throne?" said John Ball.

"It could be his son, the Duke of Lancaster."

"The most hated man in England. That would help us."

"But the true heir," Bear went on, "is the king's grandson, Richard of Bordeaux."

"The child?" said John Ball. "Better yet. That would bring even greater weakness."

"Why do you think this is the proper time for an uprising in these parts?" I heard Bear ask.

"Lord Furnival is dead," said John Ball. "There is already much confusion. Lady Furnival has summoned all the authorities from his manors. With no known heirs, she is vulnerable."

"Now, listen to me, John Ball," Bear said. "It's not for me to tell you how to act. But if we are to talk of Furnival's heirs, in my travels I've discovered something of great importance."

He spoke so low that his words became indistinct.

But I had heard enough. I drew back up the stairs.

That Bear was engaged in rebellion of some sort I could not doubt. In Stromford mere *talk* of such things was considered a hanging offense. What would happen if Bear were caught? It seemed, moreover, that he was not just a juggler, but some kind of spy.

As I lay on the pallet, I tossed and turned until I finally decided it was air I needed. Getting up, I poked the shuttered window open a little way, then glanced down upon the street. At first I thought it was deserted. Then, across the way, I saw a figure standing in the shadow of an overhanging building.

I thought of going down the steps and telling Bear. Instead, I held back. This time I would stay put as I'd been told.

As I lay back on the hay, I was determined to remain awake until Bear returned so I could tell him what I'd seen.

But the day had been long and tumultuous. Despite my intentions, I fell asleep.

42

WOKE THE NEXT MORNING to the deafening peal of bells. They were so loud, so tumultuous, for a brief moment I thought the Day of Judgment had arrived. Then I remembered I was in the town of Great Wexly with its many churches, and it was the Feast of John the Baptist. Even so, it was strange to waken in so closed a space, the air stale, the only light being that which slipped through the cracks in the shuttered window. But the pain in my wrist had gone, with only a blue mark to remind me of the attack.

I turned to Bear, wanting to tell him about the man I'd seen outside the tavern the night before. But he, taking up most of the space on the pallet, remained asleep.

To amuse myself, I plucked fleas from the straw and crushed them between my fingers. When Bear still didn't wake, I grew restless and crept out of the room, making my way down the steps to the inn's main floor.

Halfway down I stopped. The smell of wine was ripe and blended into the more embracing warmth of new baked bread. Through the open door, bright light streamed in. The rain had ceased. The tavern room was crowded.

There were tradesmen as well as peasants, men in livery, and here and there, a woman. Most people were dressed in dark and rough brown clothing, but some were very elegant in bright colors and fur trim. Midst the cloaks and hoods were hats of more variety than I could reckon.

People ate by dipping large chunks of bread into

bowls of wine, stuffing themselves, then hurrying away. The talk, loud and spoken quickly, went faster than my ear could catch. What I grasped seemed mostly about the day's market, and that it was a glorious day.

Presiding over all was Widow Daventry, louder to my ears than all the people combined. She fairly threw down loaves and bowls of drink on the tables, now and again buffeting men with her fists, or exchanging insults with a boisterous tongue, even as she put coins in her purse—the bread costing a penny, the wine the same.

As I watched, more people came in, sat and ate. Midst the swarm of people, mangy dogs wandered. I even saw a pig, snuffling up what had fallen to the ground. No one appeared to notice, or even care.

At one point I noticed a young man enter and stand at the threshold, casting his eye about the crowd. I say *eye* because I instantly recognized him as the one-eyed man we had seen in the first town in which Bear and I had performed.

I immediately backed up some steps.

His survey, however, was brief, for he turned and went.

I recalled Bear saying people would come a great distance for the market day. Even so I asked myself if it was merely accidental that he came to the Green Man's door. Could he be in search of me? Or Bear?

I hastened up to our room to tell Bear, but he was still asleep. Reluctant to wake him, I returned to the steps to stay on guard. But as I sat there, I found it impossible to escape the sensation that *something* dangerous was drawing in upon to us. It put me to mind of the snares Bear used to catch the birds we ate: an unseen loop, pulled tight, until the unsuspecting birds were caught. Perhaps we now were those birds.

43

HAD BEEN SITTING FOR I don't know how long when Widow Daventry noticed me. For a moment she stared at me as if she'd not seen me before.

"You there, boy," she called, avoiding my name, though she knew it perfectly well. "You're supposed to be in the kitchen."

Taken by surprise—for I was sure I hadn't been told I belonged there—I made no protest but came down the steps. In haste, she took me by an arm and led me away. Though one or two of the men called out, asking who I was, she did not answer.

"Where's Bear?" she asked when we entered the back room.

"Asleep."

"You mustn't be seen," she said. "He should have told you."

I made no reply, assuming Bear had told her of the attack on me, and that she felt a need to protect me. If Bear trusted her, I told myself, so should I.

I looked about. We were in a kitchen filled with food. On one side stood great barrels. From the smell of them, they contained wine or ale. Against another wall was a brick oven. There were shelves upon the walls where loaves of bread and trenchers lay. They smelled like bliss itself, enough to make my mouth water.

"Make sure the pies in the oven don't burn," the woman told me, handing me a long, shovellike wooden tool. "Place the done ones there," she said, pointing to the shelf. "There are breads ready to bake in there," she added, indicating a wooden chest.

Then she bustled out, but not before saying firmly, "And stay in here."

I peeked into the oven where the pies were baking. With the tool I'd been given, I reached in, and fetched out some. Seeing that they were not so brown as those on the shelves, I returned them to the heat.

While waiting, now and again adding more wood to the oven fire, I looked about me, amazed anew at the quantities of foods I saw. Dangling from a ceiling hook was a piece of meat as large as I had ever seen, spotted thickly with flies. Bunches of herbs—I recognized parsley, sage, and rosemary—hung from the ceiling, as did onions and leeks. Turnips and cabbages sat on shelves. Bushels of grain were there. There were clay jars and bowls aplenty, filled with I knew not what. Everything had a different smell, some pleasing, others not.

After a while I rechecked the oven. The pies were now uniformly brown. In haste, I slid them out and attempted to place them on the shelves with the others, all but scorching my hand. One was so hot it slipped from my fingers and fell to the ground, where it broke open.

In a panic, I scooped up the pieces and tried to push them together. When the bits failed to stay, I looked for a place to hide the damage, but finding none, I simply ate it, bolting the pieces like a hungry dog.

Despite my nervousness—and the speed with which I ate—I could hardly believe how rich and fine it tasted, filled with savory things I had never eaten and could not name. What's more, being hot from the oven, it filled me with a pleasing warmth.

Widow Daventry bustled in. "Have you taken the pies out?"

Feeling guilty, I said, "I put them on the shelf."

She considered them, then me. "Except for the one you ate," she said. She opened a wooden chest and took up five unbaked loaves of bread. "Bake these," she said, "but eat no more," she admonished before hurrying out.

Embarrassed, I did as I'd been told, being much more careful this time. Still, I confess, the memory of the goodness lingered for a long time in my mouth.

After a while Widow Daventry returned. "Now come with me," she said, and led me into the tavern room. It was empty of her customers. What remained were scraps of bread upon on the floor, and mostly empty tankards on the tables.

"Gather up the tankards," she commanded. "And bring them to me."

I did as I was told. She took them, sloshing out what remained onto the floor.

We worked in silence. She seemed tense. But then, as if she'd been thinking the matter over for some time, she said, "Crispin, I'm sorry for your troubles, but if ever a boy could find a good master, you've found him in Bear. As God is merciful, keep him close to his true calling—his juggling and his music. Don't let him mingle too much with those who would cause trouble. Because"—she looked at me as if I knew something I didn't—"if you don't help him, things could go much the worse for you both."

44

HEN BEAR FINALLY APPEARED, he fairly stumbled down the steps, bawling for his breakfast. He had not put on his split hat.

"Crispin," he said when he saw me standing there, broom in hand, "with the widow demanding two pennies a day for our keep, it's good to see you working. Where is the good dame?"

"In the kitchen."

"Be so kind as to fetch her."

When I did, she had me carry in two of her meat pies plus a tankard of ale, which I set before Bear.

"Ah, Widow," he said with a grin, "I'm glad the boy is toiling on our bill. For the love of Christ, all need to work honestly for their bread."

"And I trust you will too," she said.

"So I shall," he said, hand to his heart. "Except this morning I've things to which I must attend. Now, I don't want this boy out upon the town again. It will be a mercy if you keep him busy and so reduce our debt. Can you?"

Widow Daventry, who didn't look too pleased, wiped her hands on her vest. "There's always work in the kitchen. Just join me when he's done," she said to me and started from the room. At the doorway she paused.

"Are you meeting with John Ball again?" she asked.

"Widow," Bear returned severely with a glance at me, "less said, less to deny."

She glared but left us alone.

"Crispin," Bear said to me between bites of food and swallows of drink as I stood opposite him, "beyond what she tells you to do, you need to attend to your music. Practice in our room. Otherwise your sinful caterwauling will turn aside her trade.

"Now," he said, speaking softer so only I might hear, "after None—when my business is over—you and I shall leave Great Wexly."

"I want that too," I said, much relieved. "But can't I go with you this morning?"

"It's of no concern to yours. In any case you'll be safer here."

"I think someone's spying on us," I said.

"Explain yourself."

"Do you remember the first village we performed in? You teased a one-eyed man."

"Did I? How?"

"You made him angry when you toyed with his mazer. What's more, he followed us into their church. He listened when the priest told you about the boy who killed

Father Quinel. And when there was talk of the reward money, he looked at me closely. And, remember? You said we'd be here this day."

"You've been observant," said Bear attending mostly to his food. "But what of it?"

"That same young man came to the door. He looked around and went away."

"Are you sure?"

I nodded.

"Did he see you?"

"I don't think so."

Bear frowned. "If he's a spy, he's a clumsy one. If he's after you we don't need to worry. My business will be quickly done. You'll stay here and keep out of sight. Then we'll go."

"But, Bear, I think I saw someone across the alley last night, too."

"The same person?"

"I couldn't tell."

"Crispin," he said, "for one so unwilling to see the world when first we met, perhaps you notice too much now."

"You've been protecting me," I said. "Maybe I should be protecting you."

Bear looked around at me and grinned. "I like the thought. When I'm an old man I'll remind you of it. But for now, be easy."

When Bear had fairly stuffed himself with food and drunk down the remainder of his ale in one great gulp, he wiped his mouth with the back of his hand and rose up.

"Remember," he said. "This time you must stay here." Then, without any further words, he left.

I followed him out the front door and saw him stride through the crowded street.

Just to see him go off made me nervous. And sure enough, as Bear moved through the crowd, I observed the one-eyed man step out into the street and look after him.

He was not alone. A man dressed in the blue-and-gold livery of Lord Furnival's house was with him. What's more, the one-eyed man pointed in the direction Bear had taken.

I could have no doubt: the young man was after Bear, not me.

Even so, when the one-eyed man turned in my direction, I quickly ducked inside. What he might have done I didn't know, because I raced down the hall to the back door and leaped out into the alley and began to run. As soon as opportunity allowed, I went to the main street, and ran in the direction Bear had gone. I had to warn him.

45

CAUGHT SIGHT OF BEAR almost immediately. As he was so tall, his bald head all but gleaming, it was easy to follow him as he moved along the main street. Though his long strides kept him beyond my reach, I could follow without being observed.

Being the Feast of Saint John the Baptist, a market day, the streets of Great Wexly were crammed with even more people than the day before. Every alley and lane was filled. The noise was deafening.

I, who had every reason to stay unnoticed, was grateful for the crowds, and more so when I saw soldiers. Whether they were looking for me, or Bear, or just keeping order, I didn't know. I only knew I must avoid them.

Perhaps Bear saw them too, for now he plunged down a narrow side alley. I followed. Here, my pursuit proved harder, for he moved faster than before, turning this way and that, almost as if he knew I might be on his heels. Once, twice, I thought I lost him. Fortunately, his great height always gave him away.

He had gone on in this fashion for some time when I saw him duck into a building.

It was a large timbered structure, three stories high, the second and third levels leaning far over the alley upon which it faced. On the first, street level, was a large, shuttered window.

Over the door hung a board upon which an image of a boot had been painted. By this, I took it to mean that boots and shoes were made and sold there.

At first I hung back, keeping my eyes on the door to see if Bear would re-emerge. He didn't, but a few other men went in, some of them, I thought, looking furtively about as they entered. It was as if they too feared being noticed.

Nervous that Bear would be annoyed with me for disobeying his orders a second time, I decided not to go to him but remained on watch, my eyes alert for either the one-eyed man, soldiers, or men in blue-and-gold livery. But though the alleyway was full of passersby, I saw no one that gave me any reason for concern.

I was about to move on, with the thought of peeking through cracks in the building's front shutters, when another man appeared. A short man, he had a great dark cloak about him, hiding whatever clothes he wore. The hood concealed his hair. He too looked about as if to make certain no one saw what he did. Then he entered the house.

It was John Ball.

There could be no more doubt that this was more of Bear's dangerous business, from which he had warned me to keep away. I had little doubt I'd not be welcome if he discovered I was close.

Even so, my curiosity held me. As I passed the building I discovered a narrow passageway running by its further side. Pausing, I looked about to make sure I was not being observed, then slipped within it.

The passageway was narrow, but I easily made my way until I faced a rough stone wall. Having gone so far, I decided to climb it.

From the top of the wall I peered down into a

small garden of flowers and herbs. The garden was surrounded by three walls built of rough stone, the walls being not much higher than the one I'd just climbed. The back of the house served as the fourth wall. The place was deserted.

I dropped down into it.

Facing the rear of the building, I now discovered a back door had been left partially open. I started to move toward it, only to be arrested by the sound of a passionate voice which said:

". . . that no man, or woman either, shall be enslaved, but stand free and equal to one another. That all fees, obligations, and manorial rights be abolished immediately. That land must be given freely to all with a rent of no more than four pennies per acre per year. Unfair taxes must be abolished. Instead of petty tyrants, all laws shall be made by the consent of a general commons of all true and righteous men.

"Above all persons, our lawful king shall truly reign, but no privileged or corrupt parliaments or councilors.

"The church, as it exists, should be allowed to wither. Corrupt priests and bishops must be expelled from our churches. In their place will stand true and holy priests who shall have no wealth or rights above the common man. . . ."

The more I listened, the more startled I was that I understood what John Ball was saying, that he was, in fact, describing the way I had lived, and how it was wrong and could be made right. But as his words went on, I realized too how hazardous this business truly was, nothing less than rebellion against the realm of England.

Backing away from the door, I managed to climb the wall and moved hurriedly along the narrow alley toward the street. My intent was to return to the inn, there to await Bear and our departure from Great Wexly.

Before stepping from the passage between the buildings, I took the precaution of looking up and down the passageway to see if I was being observed. Which is how I spied a group of soldiers coming toward me along the street.

They were such as I had seen by the town walls: armor on their chests and rusty metal caps on their heads. Broadswords were in their hands. Daggers were at their hips.

They were being led by a man who wore a vest of

chain mail over a quilted blue jacket. In his hands he carried a crossbow. His helmet bore a crest of blue and gold. But I knew him as John Aycliffe. By his side was the one-eyed man.

46

URRIEDLY, I PULLED BACK into the narrow passageway, but peeked out, watching as the soldiers paused. The one-eyed man pointed to the sign of the boot that hung from the building into which Bear and John Ball had gone.

The moment the building was singled out, I had no doubt as to what John Aycliffe was intending.

Wasting no time, I plunged down the narrow passage between the buildings, clambered up the wall, and slipped down into the garden a second time. This time, however, I didn't pause at the rear door, but yanked it open.

I looked in upon a small room filled with benches upon which sat some seven men, Bear among them. Standing before them was John Ball.

"Bear," I shouted, "soldiers are coming!"

At the sound of my voice, he leaped up and spun about to face me. "Where?"

"On the street."

Even as I spoke, there was a great crash from the front of the house: the door being broken in.

"We are betrayed," John Ball thundered. "Save yourselves!"

There was a wild scramble for the rear door, as the men, Bear among them, raced to get out. I had to leap aside so as not to be trampled.

Once the men were in the garden, Bear took command. Using his great height and strength, he fairly lifted the men onto the back wall one by one. Once there, they swung their legs over, dropped down, and disappeared.

The last to go was John Ball.

At the top, the priest hesitated, and called: "Bear, don't lose heart. Put your faith in mighty God and me. We'll meet again tonight at the White Stag." Then he too vanished.

Bear swung about. "Crispin," he said, holding out his arms.

I ran to him. He picked me up and all but flung me

to the top of the wall. From there I looked into a narrow alley in which people were passing, one or two who looked up at me with nothing more than idle curiosity. Farther down the way—turning a corner—I could just see John Ball scurrying off.

I looked back toward Bear. He had just begun to climb the wall when the soldiers burst out of the house and into the garden.

"Go, Crispin," Bear cried. "Get out of the city. It's you they want, not me."

I dropped into the alley. But instead of running off I stood in place. Heart pounding, I strained to listening, trying to guess what was happening on the other side of the wall. What I heard were shouts: "Hold him. Secure him." Then came the sound of blows. Finally—as though from a greater distance—I heard cries, a scream, more shouts. Then, no more.

Frantic, but hardly knowing what to do—go to the aid of Bear or take care of myself—I hesitated. Guilt and fear engulfed me equally. Unable to abide not knowing what had happened, I climbed back upon the wall and looked into the garden.

It was empty.

I swung over it, dropped back down, ran toward the door and stepped inside.

The room where the meeting had taken place was a shambles. Nor was anyone there.

Opposite the door by which I'd entered was another open door. I ran through it only to find greater disorder. Several low worktables had been overturned. Shoes, slippers, and boots—in various stages of manufacture—lay scattered.

I went through another door that led me into the front room of the house. On two trestle tables, shoes and boots were displayed. And here a soldier was standing looking out the broken front door.

He turned and saw me. "Halt!" he cried.

I spun about and tore back through the rooms I'd entered, into the garden. Scrambling over the wall, I made my way along the narrow passageway by the side of the house.

Once I reached the street, I hastily looked up and down, saw that it was clear, and ran.

Whether or not the soldier came after me, I never knew. All I knew was that Bear had been taken by John Aycliffe. It was as I had feared. We'd been trapped.

47

ESPERATE TO FIND WHERE Bear was being taken, I raced wildly through the town, more than once taking the chance to stop and speak to strangers. "Did some soldiers holding a large red-bearded man go by?" I asked.

Twice, I was told that such a one had just been dragged along. What's more, they were able to point in the direction the soldiers took. I rushed on.

Then, as before, I unexpectedly burst into the great square. Though very crowded, I could see a group of soldiers crossing the far side. People were hastily making way for them.

Scrambling forward, I wove and dodged through the crowd, tables and stalls, just in time to see the soldiers—with Aycliffe—drag Bear through the open doors of a large building. It was the building I'd noticed before, the one that stood directly opposite the great church.

As soon as the soldiers entered with Bear, the doors swung shut. Armed guards, helmets and weapons bright, their livery blue and gold, took up positions before them.

Standing there, I was engulfed by alternating waves of rage and helplessness. That it should come to this! In agony, I made the sign of the cross over my heart, and made a prayer for Bear's safety. Yet I had little hope that it would bring either comfort or release for my one true friend. If only he had listened to my warning.

Then, afraid of being noticed, I stood behind a large man and peeked around him while trying to take measure of where Bear had been brought.

"What building is that?" I asked.

"The Furnivals' palace," the man replied. "And may God give grace to her Ladyship."

I continued to stare at the building as if I might see through the stone walls and discover what was happening inside. But while that, of course, proved useless, I did see a man appear on the second-level balcony, the one underneath which stone lions' heads protruded. It was John Aycliffe.

He stood looking out over the square as if in search of someone. As I gazed at him I had little doubt it was *me* he was seeking. I watched him—my heart full of loathing—until he turned and went back inside.

He had taken Bear to get at me.

Not knowing what to do, I made my way back to the Green Man. Though disconsolate, I kept my eyes alert for soldiers. I saw a few, but did not think they saw me.

Fortunately, by then I had come to know the town well enough that I reached the inn in good time. But remembering the one-eyed man, I entered through the rear.

The house was very quiet. Though I knew I should go and find Widow Daventry and tell her what had happened, I was in too much torment. I felt a need for time alone to compose myself and think what next to do. Quietly then, I crept up to the second-story solar.

As I had expected, our room was empty. But just to see Bear's sack and hat in one corner moved me greatly.

Exhausted, I lay down upon the pallet, my mind churning through a clutter of images, things, and words. Again and again the main questions returned: What would they do to Bear? What should I *do*? The truth was, I felt paralyzed.

In a spate of loneliness, I felt about inside Bear's sack, found his recorder, and played a melody. It was the first one he had taught me. But to hear it brought such sadness, I put it away. Silence was the only voice that could speak to me.

But as I lay there—I don't know for how long—I became aware of commotion. At first it appeared to come from the street. Before I could determine what it was, I heard a crash that shook the entire house.

I sat up, listening intently.

Now the tumult—shouts and cries—came from within the building itself. I heard a scream, followed by sounds of crashing, wood splintering, and I knew not what other violence.

Leaping up, I didn't know what to do until I remembered the hiding place that Bear had told me about. It took but moments for me to slip the wall board out as he had instructed. Then I crept inside the opening, taking Bear's sack and hat with me. As soon as I pulled the board back, darkness closed about me. I dared not move.

It wasn't long before I heard heavy footfalls burst into the room right beyond my hiding place. "He's not here either," I heard a voice say, followed by the sounds of breakage, and finally footsteps receding.

I pressed my ear against the wall. When I was certain no one was there, I eased my way out. The room had been completely tossed and turned. The little table had been crushed. Straw from the pallet lay strewn about.

With extreme caution, I went out into the hall. It was deserted. At the top of the steps I listened anew. From below came the sound of weeping.

48

I MADE MY WAY DOWN THE steps. When I came into the tavern room I received a further shock. The tables had been smashed. Benches were split. The serving counter was overturned. The tankards in which the ale and wine were served lay tumbled about. Many were broken.

Midst the ruins sat Widow Daventry. She was slumped and weeping. Her linen cap lay on the floor. Her hair, undone, hung down over her broad back. Her smock was torn.

Afraid to make my presence known, I stood motionless on the threshold of the room, trying to grasp what had happened. I must have made a sound, for the woman started and shifted her bulk around. She saw me and quickly turned away. But it was enough for me to see the bruises on her face, her red-rimmed eyes, her hollow mouth from which trickled a spike of blood. She gulped for air, and her crying ceased.

When I went and stood by her side, she lifted her head, looked at me, and raised a hand, once, twice, as if to pump up words. None came. It was as if she had been emptied of all life.

"Good Widow," I stammered, "what . . . happened here?"

"Soldiers," she lisped faintly. "From the palace. They're searching for you."

"Will they return?"

"Perhaps," she said wearily.

Though I quickly decided not to tell her I had been in the house, I hardly knew what to say. "If . . . they find me," I asked, hoping she would give me a different answer, "what will they do?"

"Kill you," she said. Groaning with the effort, she came to her feet and surveyed the wreckage with a dazed look. When she spied her cap upon the floor, she picked it up, and poked her fingers through its rents.

"Do you know why?" I said.

Disgusted, she tossed the cap away. "Best ask Bear."

"Bear's . . . been taken," I said.

She swung around. "By whom?"

"The soldiers."

"When?"

Diminished as she already was, my news reduced her even more. Clumsily, she righted a bench and sat down heavily. Her own weight seemed too much for her. "Tell me what happened."

I told her all.

She listened intently, muttering sacred prayers along with profanities below her breath.

When I'd done, she said, "May Jesus protect him," and made the sign of the cross. Then her shaking fingers sought her rosary beads.

I said, "What will happen to him?"

"A loving God will grant a speedy death," she said, squeezing her hands together. Tears began to run down her sunken cheeks again. With a hasty, agitated gesture, she wiped them away.

I stood there awkwardly, hardly able to breath. I said, "I heard John Ball cry out that he was betrayed."

The woman spat upon the floor. "Beware all men who confuse their righteousness with the will of God. They probably don't even know that Ball was here. It's you they want. I warned Bear."

She went back to gazing about the wreckage as if still unable to believe what she saw.

"Widow," I said, "what should I do?"

At first she didn't answer. Then she said, "You can't stay here. It's too dangerous. For you and me. They'll try to get Bear to say where you are. But even if they make him reveal where you are, since they already searched this place and didn't find you, they may not believe him. In any case, Bear will try not to say anything to harm you. He cares too much for you."

Then she added, "But even the strongest can be broken by torture."

"Torture!" I cried.

"Tonight, after curfew," she went on, "you must escape from town. In the meanwhile don't even come into this room. Stay upstairs. Did Bear show you where to hide?"

I nodded.

"Go on then. That's where you need to be."

I climbed the steps and returned to the room. After slipping inside the tiny hiding space, I closed myself in, welcoming the darkness as the only safe companion to my despair. So much bad had happened, and all because of me.

49

I DON'T KNOW HOW MUCH time passed before I heard a tapping on the board that kept me hidden.

"Open up," came Widow Daventry's whisper.

I pushed the board out. In her hands was a bowl of soup and bread.

Grateful, I took the food and began to eat, though I was almost ashamed to be so hungry.

"What have you been doing?" she asked after setting down the small candle she'd brought.

"Thinking about Bear."

"Ah," she said with a sigh. "Well you might. Crispin, forgive me being so angry with you. God knows, it's not your fault." She lapsed into silence for a while.

"Did Bear ever tell you about me?" she asked abruptly.

"No," I said.

"Two husbands. Seven children. None alive. And yet . . . I live." She reached out and rested a heavy hand on me. "Crispin," she whispered, "does God . . . have reasons?"

"I . . . don't know."

Head bowed, she began to weep again. I took her rough hand and squeezed it.

It was sometime before she could compose herself.

Cautiously, I said, "Good Widow, can you read?"

She looked at me with vacant eyes. "A little. Why do you ask?"

"Can you tell me what it says . . . here?" I held out my cross.

She took it and turned it over in her hands. "It's from the Great Sickness," she said. "I don't have to read it. Bear told me what it says."

"He did?"

She nodded. "It says, 'Crispin—son of Furnival.' "

I stared at her.

"You're Lord Furnival's son."

"How can that be?"

"Who did you think your father was?"

"My mother only said my father died before I was born. In the Great Sickness."

She shook her head. "Crispin, for these lords to have sons out of wedlock is common."

"And Bear knew about me?" I managed to say.

"Yes."

"And he told you."

She nodded. "He guessed it from this cross, and because of what happened to you." She offered the cross back to me.

I took it. "What else did Bear say?"

She sighed. "He supposed that your mother was attached to Lord Furnival's court. That she must have been some young, gentle lady who knew how to write and read. Bear imagined her some beauty, enough to catch the eye of Lord Furnival. Furnival must have brought her—no doubt against her will—to your village.

"But when she quickened with child—you—he abandoned her, leaving orders that she be held in that place. Not killed, but never allowed to leave."

"Because of . . . *me*?"

"Yes."

"Why didn't Bear tell me?"

"He wanted to protect you."

"From what?"

"Crispin," she said, "what ever noble blood there is in you, is only . . . *poison*. Lady Furnival, who's the power here, will never let you have the name. She'll look on you as her enemy, knowing that anyone who chooses to oppose her will use you and what you are."

"Does she even know of me?" I said, amazed.

When the woman said nothing, I repeated the question.

"If she knows as much as I, she may," said the widow.

"What do you mean?" I cried.

"Crispin, I can not be certain, but if the rumor of the time—thirteen years ago—was true, I believe I know who your mother was. She was the youngest daughter of Lord Douglas. Lord Furnival became infatuated with her. It was the talk of the town. Then word was given out that this young woman died. Apparently not."

"What difference does that make?" I asked bitterly. "She's dead now."

"But if Lord Douglas knew his daughter had a son by Lord Furnival, he might make a claim to the Furnival wealth through you. And if Lady Furnival knew of you as well, she would do anything to protect her power here.

"Your connection gives no honor. No position. What someone fears is not you, but that you will be used. Can't you see it? Your noble blood is the warrant for your death. It will remain so till it flows no more."

I stared at her. "Did Bear know this about my mother?"

"I did not tell him."

"Why?"

"He thought of you as his son. Why put a greater distance between you?

"Crispin, if it's any comfort, you're probably not the only possible claimant. Considering Furnival's reputation, you're probably only one of many. The House of Furnival will want you *all* dead."

"But . . . I make no claim."

"Those who know of your existence fear you will. Which is why you must get away as fast as possible and never—ever—return to these parts."

She reached out and touched me softly on the face with her rough hands. "May sweet Jesus protect you," she said before she took her leave.

50

HEN WIDOW DAVENTRY LEFT, I lay back down, and in the closeness of the hiding place, I held the cross of lead before my eyes. Though I could see nothing, I stared at it.

As I did, I began to see how my new knowledge made sense of the way my mother and I had lived for so many years.

Her words about my father. Few and bitter.

Father Quinel's saying she could read and write, but never revealing it to me.

The way people in Stromford Village looked upon us as different.

Aycliffe treating us with such contempt.

Her calling me "Asta's son," since I was all she had, and that was all she could say. But all the same, christening me secretly with my father's name.

No wonder she sometimes clung to me, and just as oft thrust me away. I was her life. She cared for me. Yet I was the cause of her destruction.

Thus we were foreigners to Stromford. Unwanted prisoners.

Then, the courier had arrived with his document, probably to announce the impending death of Lord Furnival. His protection—such as it was—was removed.

Only then did the words I heard in the forest make sense:

"And am I to act immediately?"

"It's her precise command. Are you not her kin? Do you not see the consequences if you don't?"

"A great danger to us all."

The *her* was Lady Furnival.

To say I had stolen money was merely Aycliffe's excuse to declare me a wolf's head. He sought to kill me because of who I was. No, not who *I* was, but who my father and mother were. For me—as Widow Daventry had said, they cared not so much as a rooster's tooth.

Father Quinel must have known the truth. And he was killed. Again, Aycliffe's hand.

And Bear came to know it but didn't tell me. He

was shielding me from the poison in my blood.

Now he had been taken, most likely to be killed. All because of me.

No, I had to remind myself. Not because of me, or anything I'd done, but because I was—Lord Furnival's son. The only question was, now that I knew who I was, what should I do?

Because it was clear to me that they had taken Bear to get at me.

51

OR THE REST OF THE DAY I remained in the hiding place, thinking. In doing so, I continued to piece together the fragmentary bits of my life and place them together until they became a mosaic.

I kept asking myself if I felt different, if I *was* different. The answer was always *yes*. I was no longer nothing. I had become two people—Lord Furnival's son . . . and Crispin.

How odd, I thought: it had taken my mother's

death, Father Quinel's murder, and the desire of others to kill me for me to claim a life of my own.

But what kind of life?

I supposed some might have considered me blessed in that I was of high blood. But I knew that blood, as Widow Daventry had said, to be nothing but venom. That Lord Furnival was my father had been but a cruel burden. Bear—in the short time I had known him—was a thousandfold more a faithful father to me.

For the first time, I began to think upon John Ball's words. They made sense. For what I recalled most was his saying "that no man, or woman either, shall be enslaved to any other, but stand free and equal to one another."

I recalled too, what Bear had told me, that he was a fool because he should "like to be in Heaven before he died."

I saw it then: Bear and Ball were talking about the very word Father Quinel had used, freedom. Something I had never had. Nor did anyone in my village, or the other villages through which we had passed. We lived in bondage.

To be a Furnival was to be part of that bondage.

As time passed in the darkness of my hiding place,

the one thing I knew for sure was that as Bear had helped to free me, he had given me life. Therefore I resolved to help free him—even if it cost me that new life to do so.

52

T WAS SHORTLY AFTER THE church bells rang for late-afternoon Vespers that the widow reappeared. "I've found someone to help you escape Great Wexly," she said. "You'll go tonight. The man knows a safe way over the walls. If all goes well, you'll not be seen."

"But what about Bear?"

"In the name of God, Crispin," she said, "you cannot help him. He's already lost."

She started to leave.

"Where do you think I should go?" I said.

She shrugged. "Go as far away as possible."

"Bear spoke of going to Scotland."

"Perhaps out of the kingdom is best."

"I don't know where Scotland is."

"To the north," she said.

"When will your man come?" I asked.

"After Compline—and curfew. Pray for clouds."

"Why?"

"It will be darker."

"Widow," I said as the woman moved to leave me. "Where is the White Stag?"

"By the Western Gate. Why do you ask?"

Not wishing to mention John Ball—whom she seemed to hate—I said, "Bear spoke of it."

She smiled grimly. "I'm sure Bear, God keep him, spoke of many taverns."

I fell asleep, only to waken at the sound of ringing bells. Shortly after, I heard the tramp of feet outside. Then, from some distance came the cry, "The hour of Compline is at hand. The curfew is in force. No one may be on the streets."

Not much later the widow appeared holding a lighted lamp. "The man is here. It's time."

I got up, making sure I took Bear's sack as well as his hat. I also took some of the pennies we had earned and placed them in a pocket. Lastly, I touched around my neck to make certain my leather purse was there. I did not want to leave my sole possession—the cross of lead—behind.

"Widow," I said, "I should pay for our lodging."

"Don't be foolish. You'll need whatever you have."

She led me down the steps. In the dimness of the empty tavern room, a man stood. He was rather small, with one shoulder higher than the other. His garb—jacket, leggings, and boots—was dark. He had a scabrous face, with a dirty cloth wrapped around his neck. His mouth was a narrow slit.

"God be with you," I said to him.

"And you," he said, avoiding my eyes.

Widow Daventry led us to the back door. Before she reached it she blew out the lantern. Only then did she open the door.

"The moon is full," she whispered. "Be careful. God keep you well."

"The Lord's blessings on you for your help," I returned.

Impulsively, she reached out and embraced me tightly, then with a sigh pushed me away.

I stepped into the alley. The man came close behind and shut the door behind us.

"Follow me," he said.

Without a backward look he moved away. One foot dragged, so that as he walked, he made a little scraping sound upon the ground.

I glanced up to the clear sky with its bright, full moon. Ill omen or good, it occurred to me that I might never see the sun again.

53

HE MAN WHO GUIDED ME did not speak as we moved along narrow alleys and lanes. Never once did we set foot on the main street. But once, when we heard the watch approaching, he slipped into an alcove. Breathlessly we waited until they passed.

It was then I said, "I need you to take me to the White Stag tavern."

"I was told to bring you to the walls," he said.

"Show the place to me, and I'll trouble you no more. And I'll pay you," I said, holding out some pennies.

He put out his hand, which in the moonlight showed me he had but three fingers. I dropped the coins.

For a moment he seemed to weigh the money. "It's not far," he said and limped away.

After passing through a warren of muddy lanes we came to the head of a dark alley. "There," the man said, pointing.

No light came from any building. "Where?" I asked.

"That building." He gestured to the head of the alley and a narrow structure two stories high.

I looked at it again but when I turned back to thank the man, he'd already gone. All I could hear of him was the foot scraping in the dark.

I studied the house he had pointed out. It was the moon that allowed me to make out a sign hanging over the door, which bore an image of a white stag, ghostlike in the faint light. Not only did the building seem on the verge of collapse, it appeared completely deserted.

I approached the building and rapped softly upon a stout door. There was no response.

Reluctant to leave, I put my ear to the door and

listened. I heard a sound within. Emboldened, I knocked again. The door creaked open. I saw no one, but a voice spoke, "Who is it?"

"I'm Bear's apprentice," I whispered. "He's been taken."

The door shut.

I put my ear to the door again. I was sure I heard voices. Perhaps, I thought, they were discussing what to do.

The door reopened a bit. "What's your name?" I was asked.

"Crispin."'

"Come," someone said even as the door swung open wide enough for me to slip within.

I looked around. A small candle provided little light amidst the shadows. The room was not unlike the Green Man's, but smaller, with fewer tables and benches.

I could make out five men. Their faces were indistinct, partly hidden with cowls, making it clear they did not wish to be recognized. Still, I had a vague sense that at least some of them were those who had gathered in the shoemaker's house earlier in the day.

"What brings you here?" I was asked.

I was sure it was John Ball who spoke.

"Bear has been taken," I said.

"By whom?"

"The soldiers. The ones who came to your meeting."

"Do you know where he is?"

"He was brought to the Furnivals' palace."

"Are you sure?"

"I saw him dragged in."

"God have mercy on his soul," someone else said.

"They'll torture him," said another. "They'll make him give our names."

"He doesn't know them."

"He won't inform on you," I said. "I'm sure he won't. He's too strong for that. He'd rather die."

"Braver and stronger men than Bear succumb to pain," said one of the men.

"And he's grown weak," the man I thought was John Ball said. "When we met a year ago, he was ready to join us in our brotherhood. Since then, he's altered his mind."

I said, "He says things are not ready."

"How would a juggler know about such matters?" someone asked.

"The man's a spy," John Ball said. "It's his business to know."

To hear the revelation was to know that it was true. The only part of my surprise was that I had not thought it out myself.

Then John Ball said to me, "Why did you come here?"

"I need to help Bear."

"You can't," said another. "The palace is too well guarded. Besides, they'll have put him in the dungeons."

"Boy," said John Ball, "Bear told me you're Lord Furnival's bastard son. You were most likely the reason our meeting was discovered. Didn't Bear turn away from our brotherhood? How can we be certain of your loyalties? If you had any sense you would be gone by now."

"It was I who warned you before," I said. "And it was Bear who helped you escape."

There was some uneasy shifting about by the men.

"He's lost his way," John Ball said angrily. "We can't endanger ourselves any further."

There were some low, if indistinct, murmurs of assent.

I said, "Can someone at least guide me to the square?"

"What do you think you can do?"

"I can't abandon Bear," I said.

"If it's true who you are, they probably took him as bait," said someone. "For you. You're doing exactly what they want."

"I have to try."

One of the men came forward. "I'll bring you close."

54

E REACHED THE SQUARE NOT long after the church bells rang for Matins. As soon as we arrived, the man who had guided me disappeared without a word.

I looked over the square. The bright moon revealed a field of empty tables and stalls, deserted of its trader swarms. All lay in uneasy silence, putting me in mind of the abandoned village where I had first met Bear. But here, at one end of the square, stood the palace of the Furnivals. It was huge and dark, save for two windows on the second level. There, some dim light glimmered.

Opposite, at the other side of the square, the great church rose up in all its all majesty, its stained-glass windows glowing faintly like the embers of a smoldering fire.

As I stood and listened, I heard the sound of chanting coming from the church. Priests were at their early prayers. Their blended voices rolled across the square like a rising, falling wind.

"Media vita in morte sumus:
Quem quaerimus adiutorem
Nisi te domine?
Qui pro peccatis nostris juste irascertis.
Sancte Deus . . ."

I made the sign of the cross over my heart, imploring Saint Giles to guide and help me as he had done before. Then I turned to the palace where Bear was being held.

Even as I wondered if he was alive, I spied some movement by the central doors at the lower level.

Shielding myself behind some deserted stalls and tables, I made my way closer to the palace. When I peeked out, I saw two guards standing by the main doors. One of the men was leaning back. His arms were folded over his chest, his head bent down. He gave the impression of being asleep. The other guard was pacing restlessly.

I crept closer and studied the building. It was quite clear that there would be no getting past the main-door guards. How then could I possibly find a way inside? Then I recalled seeing John Aycliffe on the balcony. Perhaps the second level was not so well guarded.

The problem was to get there.

I moved along the square so I could examine the far side of the palace building. There, other buildings crowded in. And in the moonlight, what I discovered was that between the palace and the next building there existed only a slight separation. It was hardly more than a crevice, not big enough for a man to squeeze into.

But I was still a boy.

After waiting until the restless guard moved as far away as he was likely to go, I darted forward and squeezed into the breach I'd found. It was so narrow I went in sideways.

It was too dark to see much. But I could feel around. The palace walls were jagged stone. The wall opposite was made of some rough clay or plaster.

I put down Bear's sack. If I returned I could retrieve it. If I didn't return, it wouldn't matter.

Barely able to turn about—I was like a kernel of wheat between two stones—I pressed my hands against the opposing walls. Using my fingertips to grasp small edges and bumps, I began to move slowly up. When high enough off the ground, I lifted my legs and pushed my feet against the walls so as to gain even more purchase. Straining every bit of the way, I could climb the walls like a spider.

Exactly how long it took me to reach the balcony, I don't know. It was higher than the roof of the Stromford church. Even when I reached the level of the balcony, I was not where I needed to be. The balcony jutted out beyond the building's front wall, whereas I was lodged against the side wall.

Pushing my back hard against the palace stone, while my feet pressed against the clay wall, I managed to turn about. Now I was able to wedge myself securely in place even as I freed my hands.

Just beneath the balcony, a stone carving of a lion, its jagged mouth agape, protruded. By stretching one arm to the utmost, I was able to reach the beast's lower jaw. Grasping it firmly, I released the pressure of my body from the walls.

I swung out, holding to the lion's mouth with one hand, legs dangling high above the ground and the guards below. With my other hand I stretched up and clutched the balcony itself. Now I was clinging to the balcony with one hand. I moved the other hand up so that now I dangled with two hands. Even as I swung my feet in to gain some purchase, I hauled myself up, pulling and pulling again until I had finally hoisted myself over the balcony railing. To my great relief, no one was there. As far as I could tell, the guards below hadn't seen me.

Legs shaking from my effort, I stood on the balcony and gathered my breath. Not daring to waste any time, I hurriedly crept inside through an open balcony door. In so doing, I entered a dim and narrow hall.

I neither heard nor saw anything to cause alarm. Only at the farthest end was there some feeble light.

I looked about. The area into which I'd come was nothing more than a shallow entryway. I edged forward, pausing to notice doors on either side of the little hall. I set my ear to one of them. When I heard nothing, I pushed it in.

In the faint moonlight that came through a high small window, I saw only flags on wooden poles.

I turned to the other door, listened, then pushed it open, too. Along one wall was a rack of glaives. Another wall bore broadswords. A third held some daggers.

I took up one of the daggers, then withdrew, shutting the door behind me.

I now moved toward the end of the entry hall, leaned forward to peer in—and gasped.

55

LLUMINATED BY LIGHT CAST from a few all-but-guttered candles in wall sconces was a room of vast size. It was far bigger than any room I'd ever seen before, large enough to contain more than a hundred souls. All of Stromford could have crowded in.

The wooden ceiling was decorated with carved

interlocking flowers and vines. Walls bore panel after panel, finely wrought, upon which painted images of saints had been set.

At the very far end, just opposite where I stood, was a gigantic fireplace, faced with stone and painted tiles. The dull remnants of a fire burned.

Close to this hearth, on one side of the room, was what appeared to be the stairway.

Before the hearth stood a massive, long table, with benches and chairs. The table was littered with the heaped remains of what must have been a great feast. Bones, breads, bottles, and bowls lay scattered everywhere, as if voracious giants had gathered to dine. There were mazers and trenchers, knives and napkins, goblets—things I hardly knew, and more than I could count.

In the dimness I was able to make out a number of doors set in the walls. One of these doors was open. From the room beyond, a little flickering light emerged. I went to it and, moving cautiously, peeked in.

I had come upon something very much like a church, but it was still a room. At first glance the room seemed to contain nothing but gold, gold that burned with a richness my eyes could barely absorb. These golden surfaces were encrusted with countless jewels, blues, purples and reds, jewels, which, in the flickering candlelight, seemed to pulse with a life their own. All in all, it was more wealth than I ever could have imagined existed on this earth.

At its far end was an altar upon which stood a cross of gleaming gold. Before the cross were some lighted candles that brought illumination to the room. To one side of these candles were jeweled boxes, probably containing saintly relics.

Spellbound by such magnificence, I stepped farther inside. It was then I saw that the walls and ceilings were covered with images of holy souls. Their deep, dark eyes gazed down on me with such penetrating grief and wisdom I did not doubt they peered into my very heart.

Then I realized that on the altar a single image had been placed. It had been set to the other side of the candles, opposite the relic boxes. Here, within a jewel-studded frame, Our Glorious Lady in Her flowing robes of blue was revealed. Kneeling on the ground before Her was a knight in full armor, hands clasped in prayer, his face uplifted toward the Virgin.

To my utter amazement, I recognized the face of

the knight. It was my own, the very one I'd looked upon in the stream when Bear had made me cut my hair and wash my face. But now—as sure as I knew anything—I realized I was looking upon the image of my father.

Feeling anger and curiosity, I drew closer. The kneeling man appeared so devout, so adoring of Our Lady. Yet I knew him otherwise: a lofty lord without kindness or caring for my mother. As for me, I doubted if he had had any thought at all. Just to see him in his exalted state, made me know with finality that I was not him. No, not any part. I was myself. What I had become.

Thus I sank to my knees, and putting aside the dagger, prayed that God on His throne, with my mother by His side, would judge Lord Furnival for what he truly was.

I was completely absorbed when a voice behind me said, "Who are you? What are you doing here?"

I sprang to my feet and turned about.

It was John Aycliffe.

56

YCLIFFE'S BLACK-BEARDED face, hard, sharp eyes, and frowning lips were frighteningly familiar. So was the sword at his side. The more I gazed on him, the more my panic rose and my eyes turned toward the floor.

"You," he said into the silence. "Asta's son."

Though it was a struggle to lift my eyes, I did so. His gaze showed such disdain, I could feel my wrath rise within. Here was the man who had been so cruel to my mother. Who had treated me with such contempt and wished me dead. Who had murdered Father Quinel. Who had abducted Bear.

"The wolf's head," he said. "How dare such a filthy peasant as you even presume to put your foot within this place?" He turned toward the entryway.

"If you're intending to call the guards," I said, "tell them Lord Furnival's son has come."

He halted and turned back to me. His swarthy face had become pale. "What did you say?"

"I am Crispin," I said, working to keep my gaze steady on his face. "Lord Furnival's son."

I saw him glance over my shoulder at the image of Lord Furnival, comparing me to him.

"You're nothing of the kind," he said and once again turned to go.

"You know what I've said is true," I said, hoping he wouldn't hear the quaver in my voice. "You've always known."

Again he paused. "You're not even human," was his reply.

"I've proof," I insisted.

"You can't prove what isn't so."

In haste, I took out my cross of lead from my leather pouch. "It's written here," I said, holding it up. "It was my mother's. Given to me when she died. She wrote the words on it."

"Words? What *words?*"

"It reads, 'Crispin—son of Furnival.'"

For a moment he was still. Then he said, "Anyone can write words."

"Not anyone," I said with growing anger. "It was my mother. And I believe them. As do others.

And people will need only look upon me to see who I am. And when I say I am the grandson of Lord Douglas—"

"Give that cross to me!" he cried, holding out his hand.

"No," I said. "It belongs to me."

Furious, he stepped forward and lifted a fist as though to strike me.

In response I held up my hand, using the cross that rested in my palm as a shield.

He hesitated.

"I know what happened," I said. "Lord Furnival brought my mother to Stromford. He left her there with me, making you our keeper and granting us only a living death. When Richard du Brey came to Stromford with news that my father had returned to England and was mortally ill, you were charged with killing me. It's *you* who fears me. You fear I'll become your lord."

He made no response, but his eyes told me that I was right.

"It was you who killed Father Quinel," I went on. "To keep him from telling me who I was. It was you who said I was a thief and proclaimed me a wolf's head so that any man might kill me."

"Your mother was nothing but a servant," Aycliffe said. "She was too low to reach so high. She forgot her place. It didn't serve her well. There's an order to things which God Himself has put in place. It can never be changed. How can you expect to stand against it?"

"I came for something else," I said, hardly able to contain my fury.

"Money?" he said.

"Your soldiers took a friend of mine."

He said nothing.

"He goes by the name of Bear," I continued. "A great red-bearded man."

"What about him?"

"If you'll let the two of us—both him and me—leave Great Wexly, we'll not come back. You'll never see me again."

After a moment he said, "How can I be sure?"

I lifted my trembling hand. "I'll swear it on this cross."

"You forget," he said, "you're a wolf's head. All I have to do is call the guards. Anyone may kill you. You're nothing." So saying, he turned about and stepped from the room.

I reacted by reaching down, snatching up the dagger, and leaping forward, flinging myself at his back.

I took him by such surprise that with a cry, he stumbled, tripped, and fell, crashing to the ground. Even as he struggled to reach his sword, I was on him again, knocking him down a second time.

I pressed the dagger's point into his neck. "If you call the guards, I'll kill you," I cried, pushing his face to the floor.

Panting heavily, he made no response.

Summoning all my strength, I drew the blade against his neck. Blood began to flow. "What you wanted for me," I said, "is about to happen to you."

"Will you," he whispered desperately, "swear upon that cross and in the name of God, that if I let you and this man go, you'll never come back and make no claim upon the house of Furnival?"

"Willingly."

"And you'll give me that cross?"

"When we have passed through the city gates." Even as I spoke I worked to keep my hand steady so he never ceased to feel the pressure of the dagger's point. "But you," I said, "must swear first."

"I . . . will," he said, as though it was a painful thing to say.

I released him.

He sat up, and touched his neck, looking at the blood that smeared his fingers.

"Swear," I said holding up the cross of lead but keeping the dagger near.

He hesitated, but then he said, "In the sacred name of Jesus, I, John Aycliffe, swear that I shall allow you—Asta's son—and the man called Bear, to leave this city insofar as you have sworn never to return, never to claim Lord Furnival to be your father and to leave the cross with me."

Then I said, "In the name of the Father, the Son and the Holy Ghost, I, Crispin, do swear that if you let Bear go, he and I will leave Great Wexly and never return. Nor will I ever make claim that Lord Furnival was my father. Furthermore, once out of the city I'll give you the cross.

"Now," I said, "take me to Bear."

His reply was to gaze at me with eyes full of hate. But then he got to his feet and began to walk away, saying, "Follow me."

57

ARELY BELIEVING I HAD persuaded John Aycliffe to do as I wished, I held the dagger in one hand even as I clutched the cross of lead in my other. By one or the other I was determined to succeed.

Pausing briefly to take up a candle from one of the wall sconces, the steward proceeded to go down the steps I had noticed in the corner of the great room. To my great relief, he left his sword where it lay on the floor.

The steps were very wide, winding down and around to the lower floor. Upon reaching the bottom we came into a large, enclosed room with many shelves and two large tables. In the dim light, it appeared to be some kind of pantry. There were stacks of flat breads, mazers, bowls, and jars in abundance.

Aycliffe continued into a hallway. In this place the walls were covered with great tapestries. Here too, for the first time, we came upon others. Who exactly they were, or what service they performed, I couldn't tell. They lay stretched out on the floor, asleep.

Having never seen so large and magnificent a dwelling, it was all I could do to keep my eyes on Aycliffe as he passed through what appeared to be yet another pantry. In this place great quantities of food were stored, so much more than I had seen at the Green Man. We saw more servants too, but as before, they lay asleep, this time in a corner.

The steward went to another corner stairway, this one made of stone. These steps plunged down steeply. Whatever warmth there had been faded quickly. The deeper we went, the colder and damper it became.

Sputtering, smoky torches had been set in wall holes every few feet. A few men were sitting on the steps, while others lay sprawled sleeping. No matter who they were, as soon the steward appeared they leaped up and saluted him.

Only when we reached the foot of the steps did Aycliffe pause. We had come to a large, almost round area constructed of stone from the floors to the low, vaulted ceilings.

Coming quickly to the fore was a man whom I recognized as one of those who had attacked me the night before. There was a puzzled look upon his face when he saw me, but he nevertheless bowed to Aycliffe.

"Sir—" he started to say.

Aycliffe interrupted. "Take me to where the red-bearded man is."

The soldier took up a smoky torch and led the way.

We were now moving through cellar regions, through one narrow passage after another. The ceilings were soot-blackened. The air was close and foul. Puddles of stagnant water lay underfoot. The walls were streaked with green.

"He's here, sir," the soldier said. We had come to a small door set into the wall.

"Unlock it," Aycliffe commanded.

The man produced a ring of keys, selected a large one, applied it to the lock and pulled the door open.

"You may enter," he said to me.

I hesitated, thinking I'd be trapped inside.

Aycliffe seemed to understand my thoughts. "I've made my vow," he said as though to rebuke me. "You'll not be detained."

I reached for the torch the man held. Before he

released it he looked to the steward. When Aycliffe nodded, I was allowed to take the light.

Small as I was, I had to stoop to enter the room. It was small, dark, and stinking within. By the light of the torch I saw Bear. His great bulk had been stretched upright upon a ladderlike structure, arms bound high over his head, unshod feet bound below just as tightly. Almost naked, his bloodstained body was striped and welted as if had been whipped. His head hung limp upon his chest, his beard spread like a rumpled napkin.

"Bear?" I said.

He made no response.

"Bear," I called again, louder.

When he still made no answer I could only find the breath to say, "Bear, are you alive?"

When he gave no reply I drew closer, holding the torch near to him. Only then did I see the slight rise and fall of his chest.

Jamming the torch end into a crevice in the stone floor, I used my dagger to cut his bonds free, starting with his feet. By climbing the ladder, I released his hands, first one, then the other. Once free, he slid down to the floor, where he lay in a heap.

On my knees by his side, I took up one of his hands. It was cut and very raw. "Bear," I said. "It's me. Crispin. *Crispin,*" I repeated even louder.

Gradually Bear lifted his head. His face was so bruised it took a moment for him to open his eyes. Or only one eye, for the other was swollen shut. At first he merely gazed at me, uncomprehending, repeatedly blinking.

"Crispin?" His broken lips managed a hoarse whisper.

"I'm here, Bear," I said.

He continued to gaze at me as if not sure who I was.

Then he said, "Crispin . . . I do love you like a son. Did . . . did I betray you?"

"No, Bear, you didn't. And now you're to be set free."

When he didn't seem to understand, I took up his raw hand and gently pulled at it. "Can you come, Bear? Can you walk? We're going to leave Great Wexly. The steward swore a sacred oath to let us go."

He let out a deep sigh of exhaustion.

"Bear, you must come with me," I urged as much as begged, pulling at him again.

"Have they caught you too?" he said between parched lips.

"I'm not caught, Bear. We're both leaving. To go free. But you have to come. Now. You *must* move yourself."

At last he seemed to understand. Letting forth a great sigh, he summoned enough strength to heave himself up to his hands and knees. Then he began to crawl after me toward the entryway.

I left the little room first. Bear followed. When he came out, he managed to only just squeeze through.

By the time we emerged a ring of soldiers had gathered and were looking on in hostile silence. Aycliffe, I saw, had found a sword. It was in his hand.

I stood up. But when Bear remained on his hands and knees I knelt before him. "Can you stand?" I said, holding out my hand. He reached up, and grasped it.

"He needs help," I said. "Get him some water."

No one moved.

"Help him," I commanded.

All eyes went to Aycliffe. He gave a small nod. Three of the men stepped forward, and reached out to Bear. But when they touched him, he reared back like a wounded beast, and with a spurt of energy struck away their hands.

"Crispin," he called.

I went before him. He looked up—seemingly to make sure it was me—then lifted one of his long arms, and set it on my shoulder. By sheer strength of will, he began to pull himself up, leaning much of his weight on me. When he finally stood, I could see how cruelly battered he was. Yet he was still large enough so that some of those looking on stepped back in awe.

I was handed a jug of water, which I passed on to Bear. He clutched it in both hands, and drank from it deeply, then let the rest cascade over his head and body. That done he flung it away, letting the jug smash. The water helped him, though his breath was still labored. He stood somewhat taller. He had managed to open his other eye, if only partly.

"He needs some clothing," I said.

Once again all eyes went to Aycliffe, who nodded.

One of the men came forward, offering me a cloak. I placed it around Bear's shoulders.

"Put a hand on my shoulder," I said to him. "We're leaving."

Bear, standing behind me, did as I bid. But before me, in a semicircle, stood the steward and some ten other men. All were armed.

I took a step forward. No one moved.

Heart hammering, I lifted my hand, the one that held the cross of lead. "Shall I read what is written here?" I said directly to Aycliffe.

Bear's hand tightened slightly on my shoulder.

"Shall I?" I repeated.

For a moment there was no reply. Then the steward said, "You must give it to me."

"You swore a vow to let us go first," I said.

He said, "When you give it to me, you'll go free."

I shook my head. "Once we're beyond the walls, you'll have it."

"I could kill you here," he said. "Both of you."

"This man made a sacred vow to let us go," I said loudly. "He did so on this cross."

With all looking at him, Aycliffe seemed unsure what to do.

Then I said, "Shall I tell them who I am?"

The steward didn't reply. In the silence I was sure all could have heard my heart hammering.

Then Aycliffe said, "I'll take them to the city gates."

The men stepped to either side, allowing us a narrow passage.

Aycliffe took the lead. I followed. Bear, his hand still resting on my shoulder, shuffled right behind me. I turned to look at him but could not read his emotions.

Moving slowly, we made our way through the cellar regions, then to the steps. Once there, I offered myself as a crutch to Bear, which he accepted, though I sensed that he was regaining something of his old strength. Even so, the climb was slow and painful. When we reached the first level I could hear, if only dimly, church bells ringing. I wondered if they were tolling a call to arms or to prayer.

More soldiers were on guard at the front door. When they didn't move, we all stopped.

"Give me the cross," Aycliffe demanded.

"On your vow. Not until we're safely past the city gates."

"Open the doors," he said angrily.

The soldiers pushed open the doors.

It was, as I had prayed, dawn.

As we stepped out from the palace, the town's

church bells were still ringing. Above the square, a whirl of agitated black birds circled through the air. Before us, traders were setting up their wares in stalls and tables. Those closest to us stopped their work and stared.

Bear and I went forward. Aycliffe stayed with us as did an escort of some seven soldiers.

"Wait," I cried. I ran to the side of the palace and took up Bear's sack, then rejoined him.

"Take us to the gates," I said to Aycliffe.

Though his look was full of hatred, the steward turned and began to move along the stone-paved road. We went slowly, a troop of soldiers all around us, while I wondered if they would truly let us go.

58

S WE WENT ALONG, PASSERSBY stopped and gawked at us in silence. Others followed in our wake. "I have a dagger," I whispered to Bear as we approached the town gates.

"Give it to me," he said and came close against my side. When he did I slipped the dagger from my pocket and gave it to him. He took it in his great hand, concealing it in the folds of his cloak.

We reached the city gates. Though they were open, they were guarded by soldiers.

Aycliffe paused and turned. In one hand he held his sword. In his other hand he had a dagger.

"Let us pass," I called out to Aycliffe.

In response he shouted so all could hear: "Both of you are traitors. And by my honor you'll go no farther. I may have made a vow to let you go. But this boy has been proclaimed a wolf's head. No one else is bound by my oath. Anyone may slay him. I'll give a pound reward to anyone who slays this wretched boy here and now."

I shrank close to Bear. It was he who cried out to Aycliffe, "Coward! Traitor!"

"It's not you I want," the steward said. "It's the boy. He's vexed me long enough. Leave him, and you can have the reward."

In response, Bear shoved me behind him so he faced the steward. His cloak had fallen away. In the morning's early light his huge body was filthier, more bloody than I had realized. Whip and burn marks scored his chest and arms. But the dagger was in his hand.

"Son of Lucifer," he cried to Aycliffe. "Oath breaker! Murderer!"

I glanced around. The soldiers, swords in hand, had formed a semicircle behind us.

Before us it was much the same. Aycliffe stood unmoving, soldiers right behind him. Quickly, they shifted so that we—the steward, Bear and I—were completely surrounded. Some of the soldiers were grinning, so eager were they to watch us die.

Beyond them, townspeople gathered too and gawked.

Now the steward moved forward. His broad sword was extended and moved from side to side. The hand that held the dagger he kept wide. I tried to keep out of the way.

Bear, with just the dagger held before him, remained unmoving, gazing at our enemy.

Aycliffe made a thrust with his sword, which Bear stopped with a sudden movement of his dagger. The metal clashed loudly. From those around us, I heard a collective intake of breath.

His stroke gone amiss, the steward backed away. Then the two men, breathing hard, eyed one another.

Aycliffe made a series of lunges, first one way, then another, which Bear managed to beat off, but only because he retreated.

Aycliffe paused again.

It was Bear who now attacked, trying to slip sideways to the steward's dagger side, while making a dive at the man's body. Now the steward swung wildly around with his broadsword, forcing Bear back.

Once again the two men paused while trying to decide their next move.

It was the steward who made the next series of thrusts. These Bear avoided, but I could see that he was tiring. Not only was he on the defensive, he was gradually being edged back toward the soldiers who had lifted their swords up to make a wall of deadly spikes.

Bear tried to move forward, but Aycliffe swung out wildly.

"Bear!" I shouted. "There are soldiers behind you."

Whether he heard me or not, Bear tried to press back upon the steward. While he made some progress, it was very little. And now, as if some signal had passed between Aycliffe and the ring of soldiers, they began to creep forward, making the spiked circle smaller and smaller.

It was then that Aycliffe swung hard while lunging. In doing so he struck the dagger clear out of Bear's hand. The blade skittered across the stones. Bear made a move toward it, but was blocked by the steward and his blades. Then Aycliffe began to close in on Bear.

But with all eyes on the two of them, I ran forward and snatched up the dagger.

"Bear, I have the dagger!" I shouted.

Hearing me, the steward swung about. Seeing me with the dagger, he raised his sword high, prepared to bring it down on me. At that moment Bear leaped forward. With his great arms he hugged Aycliffe, pinning the steward's arms to his sides. The steward struggled to free himself, but Bear squeezed tighter and tighter, grunting like an animal, until the steward's sword and dagger fell to the ground with a double clang.

Then Bear picked up the steward, held him over his head, and flung him bodily through the air at the soldiers. It happened so quickly the soldiers had no time to react.

Aycliffe was impaled on the soldier's swords, run clear through by several points.

I gasped with horror. From the onlookers too, there was a great shout of terror.

The soldiers, stunned, and very frightened, moved back several steps as Aycliffe rolled back on the stone road, twitched, kicked, and became very still in his own pooling blood.

No one moved.

Then Bear, panting hard, snatched up the steward's dagger and sword and brandished them at the soldiers who stood before the city gate. "Make way for us," he bellowed, "or by Saint Barnabas, you'll meet the selfsame fate."

The soldiers and the crowd slunk back. The way to the gates was clear.

"Crispin, hurry!" cried Bear.

I ran where the steward lay. From around my neck, I removed the cross of lead and laid it on the steward's bloody chest.

With all eyes upon us, Bear and I walked out through the gate. Not one said a word. Neither Bear nor I spoke. I could hardly believe what had happened.

"Crispin," said Bear as we moved away from the walls, "in that place they had me, I heard chants coming from the cathedral. The priests were singing, *'Media vita in morte summas,'* which means, 'In the midst of life there is death.' But, Crispin," he said, "can't you see the new truth we've made? In the midst of death there's life!"

I laughed and we embraced. Then, as we moved along the road, I swung Bear's sack around and pulled out his two-pointed hat, and leaping up, I plopped it on his head, albeit crookedly. But he removed the hat and then put it on *my* head.

"I, Bear of York," he roared, loud enough for all the world to hear, "do dub this boy, Crispin of Stromford, a full member of the guild of free men. In so being, he is free of all obligations save to his God."

I took out the recorder. When I began to play, Bear laughed. Then he began to sing. Though he did not sing in his usual bellowing voice, it was his voice all the same:

"Lady Fortune is friend and foe.
Of poor she makes rich and rich poor also.
Turns misery to prosperity
And wellness unto woe.

So let no man trust this lady

Who turns her wheel ever so!"

Then, as I played the pipe and Bear beat his drum, we two cantered forward on our journey.

And by the ever-loving God who sits above, my heart was full of more joy than I had ever felt before. I was unfettered, alive to an earth I hardly knew but was eager to explore. What's more, I knew that feeling to be my new-found soul, a soul that lived in freedom. And my name—I knew with all my heart—was Crispin.